Legend of Promise

To Annetta
Thanks My
Friend and
God Bless You!
Delores Leggett Walker

Legend of Promise

A Novel

Delores Leggett Walker

Promise Series

Book One

Dream Publication

DP - Dream Publication

Legend of Promise

Copyright © 2013 by Delores Leggett Walker
This title is also available as a Kindle ebook.
Cover design by Jack Howdeshell
Line editor: Toni Garland

This book is a work of fiction. Names, characters, places, and incidents either are products of the author's imagination or are used factiously. Any resemblance to actual events or locales or persons, living or dead, is entirely coincidental.

Printed in the United States

Library of Congress Cataloging in Publication Data
Walker, Delores Leggett
     Legend of Promise / Delores Leggett Walker
          p. cm. – (Promise Series; bk. 1)
     ISBN-9781492252740

Christian Fiction /Suspense

Dedication

This book is lovingly dedicated to the
Heavenly Father
who placed the dream in my heart
and to those who caught the dream with me . . .
you know who you are.

It is also dedicated to my Daddy, Theodore Leggett,
who was the best storyteller I have ever known.

Author's Note

I have been a journalist all of my life. I started my career at the age of three when my neighbor allowed me to interview her at our weekly tea parties. I became an actual reporter in my early fifties when I was hired to cover news for my hometown newspaper, Mayo Free Press. I have always been at home in the newsroom, whether it was at someone's kitchen table or in the sophisticated setting of a twenty-first century newspaper.

Although I retired seven years ago, I continue to be a journalist and still write a weekly column, 'Let's Talk,' for Perry News Herald. I owe a lot to journalism. It gave me a chance to share my love of writing through weekly news coverage as well as my Daddy's stories. He inspired me to believe that everyone has a story to tell and that there will always be those who will enjoy reading them.

Stories can be born from memories, a casual statement by someone or in this case by an heirloom quilt passed down in my husband's family since the Civil War. The beautiful Double-Wedding Ring Quilt that is the inspiration for this book was made by Georgiana Sullivan Walker in the 1800's. She gave it to her grandson, J.L. (Dock) Walker before her death in 1918. He passed it to our daughter, Vickie before his death in 1992.

The quilt and its origin are factual, but the Legend is my own making.

Prologue

Peron, Georgia -- June 1861

A knock shattered the hushed quiet of the early morning. Georgiana's and Alice's hands stilled on the patchwork quilt that lay on the quilting frame between them.

"Please see who it is, Alice," Georgiana softly said.

"Okay," she whispered, as she hesitantly rose, walked to the front of the small house and opened the door.

A moment later, Georgiana heard the voice of Pastor Smith telling Alice to close the door quickly and lock it. "I may have been followed," he said.

A look of fear tightened the black skin of Alice's face. She stood motionless; barely daring to breathe as she saw the Pastor push the curtain back slightly, to see if anyone had followed him.

Georgiana had lain the quilt aside when Pastor Smith had rushed in. She didn't speak until he joined her near the quilting frame.

"Pastor, what on earth is going on?"

He took her outstretched hands in his and said, "Georgiana, I don't mean to frighten you. Sit down, please. I need to talk with you."

Georgiana shook her head as if to drive away her fear. "Yes, of course. Where are my manners? Would you like a cup of tea?"

"No, thank you. There is something I need to tell you," he said as he glanced over his shoulder at Alice who was still standing near the door.

Georgiana saw his look and said, "Go ahead, Pastor. You know I have no secrets from Alice."

Pastor Smith turned and offered Alice his hand. She looked to Georgiana for assurance and saw her slightly nod her head before she placed her hand in his. He drew her into the circle as he took Georgiana's hand again, and asked them to join him in prayer.

"God in heaven, I bow humbly before you and ask you to guide our steps as we carry out the plan placed in our hands. Amen."

With their hands still held in his, he told them what had happened, as he was praying last evening. "I was asking God to be merciful to our Nation that is becoming more and more divided by this horrible war. I felt the warmth of a presence in front of me. I looked up and saw a beautiful being surrounded with light; I believe it was an angel. He gave me three tiny seeds and told me there is life in the seeds. Georgiana, he said that I should bring them to you and Alice. He said you would protect them for a time when the world would be in chaos again, and would need the protection of a merciful God. I told him I didn't understand. The world is in chaos now. If they could make a difference, why would God choose not to use them now?"

Squaring his shoulders, he reached in his coat pocket and found the seeds. He opened his hand and said, "I have done what God asked of me. It is in your hands now, Georgiana."

One

Monroe, Florida -- 2013

Loren Taylor stared at the red roses of the family wreath that rested on top of Grammas' casket. Her petite body trembled as she lifted tear-filled eyes to the blue sky that framed the solemn scene. The two were at odds; the casket spoke of an ending, the clear sky shined with the promise of a beginning.

"I feel so broken and alone." She sobbed with gut-wrenching cries that tore at her self control as she clutched the hands of her best friends, Carolyn and Leta.

They stroked her hands, gently offering whatever comfort they could with kind words, as Loren passed through one of the most difficult storms of her life.

"You're not alone, Loren. We're right here with you," Carolyn soothed, her own face covered with tears.

"I know, and I am so grateful for your friendship. I couldn't have gone through the last four days without you and Leta. It's just happened so suddenly. This time last week Gramma was laughing about me finally being a grown-up, and now she's gone."

Her friends exchanged an understanding look with each other as Loren reached out her hand to touch Grammas' final resting place. They stood and pulled her into their arms. Even though they wanted to stay with her, they knew she needed time alone with Gramma Lil.

"We're going to wait for you in the car. Take all the time you need," Leta said.

Loren shook her head in answer, and watched them walk to the car. Turning to the casket, she placed her hand on it, needing to feel close to the person who rested there. She broke one of the roses from the wreath and inhaled the fragrant smell, "Gramma, this is really hard for me. I need you. I'm not ready to be a grown-up."

I'm here . . . whispered on the wind. The smell of the rose intensified. Loren straightened and looked around. She was alone...but yet... she wasn't alone...she knew her Grammas' voice. Her blue-grey eyes, the color of the morning mist, lingered on the casket. In the midst of her sorrow, Gramma had managed to comfort her – to let her know that she would always be near – that she was as close as the memories they had made together, and that life would continue, even though they were apart for the time being.

Stronger now, Loren said, "I love you, Gramma. I won't say goodbye. I know it's only a parting of our ways for the moment. We'll be together again one day."

Loren opened Grammas' Bible that she had held during the memorial and pressed the rose between the pages. She hugged it close to her.

14

She walked away, knowing God would provide all that she needed. It was how Gramma had raised her. She would not desert her faith now. There was a life God had prepared for her. It was time to embrace it with confidence.

Carolyn and Leta sat quietly in the front seat. Loren opened the back door and slipped inside. They watched her glance back at the flower-laden casket. Leta turned to her, reached for her hand, and said, "Are you ready to go home?"

"Yes, I'm ready. I may be leaving Grammas' body to be buried but that doesn't mean she won't be with me."

Loren patted her chest, "Her words are here in my heart. They will guide me as I start this part of my journey in life."

On the drive to Gramma Lil's house, Loren told them she had decided to sell. "It's what Gramma wanted. She knew I couldn't live there with her gone. I'll collect the things I want to keep. The rest of the furnishing can go with the house."

When Leta parked the car, they followed Loren up the sidewalk to the front porch.

"Would you look at these flowers? Its early spring and her yard is already blooming with color."

"You're right, Leta. Gramma Lil was an expert gardener. She could put what looked like a dead plant in the ground and bring it back to life," Loren said.

"I imagine God will assign her to tend the flowers in Heaven."

"That would suit her just fine," Loren said with a smile as she thought about Gramma working with the flowers in heaven, without worrying about the weeds.

She turned the key in the front door with a quick twist of her hand, and stepped inside. The memories of the night Gramma died flooded her mind. Today was the first time she had been to the house since that night. Carolyn had insisted she stay with her until after the funeral. She glanced around the rooms. The smell of apples and cinnamon from the scented candles on the fireplace mantle was familiar. The comfortable over-stuffed couch in wine and pale green that bordered between old and antique sat in the same place. Everything was just like it was when she'd left, but Loren knew it wasn't the same. The heart and soul of her home was gone.

Carolyn took her hand, "I know it's hard but we're here with you."

She took deep breaths to calm her turbulent emotions. Wiping the tears that pooled in her eyes with her hand, she glanced around the room. A childlike drawing framed on the wall, caught her eye. She went over and took it down.

"Do you remember this?"

Leta took the drawing from her, looked at the three stick people and laughed, "I remember the day you drew this. It was the first day of kindergarten, and the day we met. We pledged to be friends forever. Your Gramma bragged about what a talented artist you were. She framed it, and told us it was a *milestone memory* in our lives. It has hung in this same place for eighteen years."

Loren smiled as she thought about her first day of school. "I was so scared to leave Gramma. I walked into the classroom, hanging on to her for dear life. Then the two of you danced over to me and declared we were friends. It changed my life forever, and I love you for being there on that day, and for being here today."

Leta handed the drawing back to Loren. "Okay, now, Loren, tell us what we can do. I need to leave for Tallahassee early tomorrow, and I'd like to help you as much as I can today."

"Let's start in the kitchen, "Loren said.

When she went into the kitchen, she picked up one of the cups that Gramma kept on the counter. They were used for the 'cup of tea' she'd enjoyed every morning. Seeing the sad look on Loren's face, Carolyn put her arm around her shoulders and squeezed her tightly. "Oh, honey, it's all right. Leta and I can do this. We'll clear out the cabinets and pack this up. We can label it so that you can decide what to do with it later. You go on to your bedroom and pack what you're taking from there. Go on, we've got this," she said pushing her gently.

When she opened the door to her bedroom, she paused, letting her gaze roam over the red walls and black and white checked coverlet and valences. She looked at the shelf above the windows that held her trophies and awards from her school years.

Gramma was so proud of me.

Shaking off the memories that threaten to bring fresh tears, Loren began packing her clothes and keepsakes. She labeled each one and dragged them to the front door. The rest of her clothes and personal items went in the set of luggage that had been a graduation present from Gramma.

She slipped down the hall to Grammas' room. The door was closed. She leaned her forehead against the door for a moment before opening it. The sweet smell of her rose and honeysuckle perfume still lingered in the air. The pain of her loss was hammering at her control. Gramma had raised her to face life with bravery, but this was just about more than she could bear.

"I can do this," she whispered as she put one foot in front of the other, until she stood near the bed. Flashes of memory from the horrible night when she'd discovered Gramma gasping for breath filled her mind. With resolve, she sat on the edge of the bed and ran her hands across the flowered spread.

Little by little, she thought back over her twenty-three years. The first year was blank except for the photographs and the things Gramma had told her. She had said Loren was a special surprise, coming ten months after her daughter Grace had married Bob Taylor. Their joy at her arrival, and the happiness of her first year, was recorded in photographs by her Daddy. But, the happiness was short lived when a home invasion robbed her of her parents.

Gramma said an officer knocked on her door shortly after two o'clock in the morning to tell her that her daughter and son-in-law had been murdered. Police found the men who had committed the heinous crime. A high-speed pursuit ended when the fleeing men crashed their truck in a fiery blaze over an embankment.

She told Loren, *justice was served* but Loren had wondered if it was payment enough for her loss. Gramma would not allow her to wallow in anger, telling her, "Life has some rough spots, baby girl, don't let those rough spots turn into places that won't heal."

When she'd complained about life being unfair, Gramma had pulled her close and whispered, "Life is what it is. It's how we cope with it that makes the difference."

A tap on the door brought Loren back from her memories. Carolyn stuck her head around the door and whispered, "Are you okay?"

"Just give me a minute. I'm coming."

"We'll wait on the porch. The boxes are packed and by the door."

"Thanks. I'll be right out."

She listened to their footsteps, and heard the front door open and close. Taking a final look at the room, Loren hesitated, listening with her heart.

I'm here.

Loren closed her eyes and whispered, "I know, Gramma. I will survive this. You taught me well. I'll make you proud. I promise."

For the first time in almost a week, she knew that she would be able to move forward. The paralyzing numbness had left. In its place were strength, and a resolve that told her life was worth living again. Today was the first day of the rest of her life. It was up to her to make it a good one. Loren left the room without looking back.

Carolyn and Leta searched her face with concern as she met them on the porch.

Loren smiled. "Look at you two worry warts. Quit frowning, I'm okay."

"Are you sure?" Carolyn asked.

"I'm sure. All the boxes are near the door. The movers will bring them to my apartment later. Oh, one more thing, can you sell the house for me?"

Carolyn nodded, "Yes, of course, I can do that."

Loren locked the front door and dropped the house key in her coat pocket. Carolyn and Leta gave her another hug before leaving. Loren waved to them, as she walked to her car that was parked in the driveway.

After they'd left, she looked at the house, and noticed how the afternoon shadows outlined it, and then slowly drifted across the yard.

Loren choked back tears. Even though she was planning to move, this was different. She could have visited, but now, Gramma would never be here to welcome her again. This was a final goodbye to her childhood home. It was the way life was, a chapter closes and another one opens.

Loren smiled and said, "Yes Gramma, I understand. Life is like the shadows: they frame our lives for a moment, and then they're gone, leaving only *the memory* of what once was there. The beauty of this is what we learn from each moment that touches our lives. Life constantly changes, moving us forward, yet allowing us to hold on to what we've learned in the moments that are gone."

Loren put her suitcase in the trunk of her car. She knew her grieving wasn't over, but she was ready to see what lay on the other side of this tragedy. It's what Gramma would tell her to do if she was still here.

Two

The drive was uneventful, traffic sparse, giving her time to compose herself before she reached her new apartment. Making a right turn on Laurel Street, she pulled into parking space twenty-three. She knew it was not a coincidence that she had parking space twenty-three. It was her present age and she took comfort in knowing that God knew exactly where she was.

Her move had been in the making since her graduation three months ago, with Grammas' approval. 'Find your way in the world, baby girl,' had been her advice. She had told her to surround herself with things that spoke to her heart. Then she added, "Don't think you are abandoning me. I'm old enough to take care of myself."

Loren marveled at the store of common sense Gramma had imparted to her. She knew Gramma had prepared her to be the best at whatever she chose to do.

With the car locked, she walked the short distance to her second-story apartment. She unlocked the door, went in and glanced at her watch. It was two o'clock. Delivery of her new furniture was set for three. She felt a bubble of excitement and danced a quick two-step around the empty room at the thought of her *just right* furniture she had bought last week. Her gaze scanned the room, mentally arranging the furniture.

A sign advertising a close-out sale at Faber's Fine Furniture had made her stop to investigate. The decision had been a good one. She had found exactly what she had wanted to match her recently painted apartment, all at half-price!

She and Gramma had found the apartment two months ago, but the move had been delayed until the other renters had left, and the repainting had been finished. The soft sand color on the walls with pristine white trim, complimented the darker sand shade of the floor tiles. It was the ideal frame for the *beachy theme* she wanted.

Sitting on the floor in the middle of the room, she visualized the natural wicker, with its big, cushy seating in tropical sea-foam green, yellow and salmon that she had chosen for the living room. The glass-top tables would hold a variety of green plants, creating a peaceful haven.

Glancing toward the open door to the bedroom, she pictured the queen-size bed in driftwood-grey wicker, with its matching chest and dresser with glass-top surfaces. She would cover the surfaces with sea-shells she had collected. A delicate pink coverlet and assorted pillows in green and yellow would complete the room, tying it all together. She loved it!

Loren wanted her space to shout her love of the warm gulf water bordering her hometown of Monroe, in Northwest Florida.

A round oak dining table and ladder-back chairs, in the corner of the dining room, were a gift from Gramma.

They had brought it over as soon as the landlord had given her the key.

The table, in rich yellow-grain of Southern Oak, went well with the chairs. They were not new, but had an old-world appeal pleasing to the eye. Polishing the wood until it shone, Loren had placed a basket of shells in the center of the table.

Looking at the table brought back sweet memories of the day she and Gramma had purchased it.

They had found the table while walking along the waterfront to burn off the calories from lunch at their favorite restaurant, Red's Seafood. The salty smell of the gulf had been carried on the gentle breeze, caressing their faces. They had spotted the table at the same time as it was carried through the door of Vic's Antique Shop. They yelled together, "Hey, that's the table!" Laughing together, they locked arms and Gramma said, "Hurry, let's go buy it."

They had made the purchase and Vic, the owner of the shop had said he would deliver it to Loren's apartment when she was ready for it. He also told them the story of why he had the table. He said he had bought it at an estate sale, up the coast at Apalachicola, from a ninety-year-old lady, who was the last surviving member of her family. Her husband and two children had died during a flu outbreak in the 1940's. Her recent move to an assisted living facility had made it necessary to let the table that she had had since she was a bride be sold, even though it broke her heart to do so. Her one request was that he would sell it to someone who would cherish it as she had. Loren and Gramma had assured him it was, love at first sight, and would be lovingly cared for.

The doorbell chimed, bringing Loren back to the present. A look in the peep-hole showed the smiling faces of Billy and Skip with her furniture delivery from Faber's. She opened the door.

"Hey Loren, got some pretty stuff for you. Direct us to the right spot," Billy said as he and Skip wiggled the couch through the door.

"In front of the window is good, Billy."

Ten trips later, the furniture was in place. Billy and Skip had been such a big help in pushing things into the right positions, saving Loren from having to deal with sore muscles later on from doing it all by herself.

"Would you and Skip like a bottle of water?"

"Water is just what we need," Billy said as he passed one over to Skip.

Taking the next bottle from Loren, Billy took a thirsty swallow before telling Loren he was sad to hear of her Grammas' death. "She was a fine lady."

Loren fought the tears forming in her eyes, "Yes, she was a fine lady."

They spent a few minutes talking about the memorial service, and the advantage of living in a small community where neighbors care enough to support each other through good times and times of sorrow.

A final check showed everything was in place, so Loren thanked Billy and Skip for all their help, and walked with them to the door and said goodbye.

With the new furniture surrounding her, Loren was in the difficult place of in-between what was familiar and what was not familiar. She was standing on the threshold of the rest of her life, and she knew she had to make the decision to move forward soon. But, for just a few moments longer, she needed to hold on to the familiarity of the life she knew best. She sat on her beautiful new sofa, closed her eyes and remembered the night Gramma died.

. . .

Her suspicion that Gramma was not as well as she wanted her to think, was confirmed when they went to see Dr. Bailey for Grammas' yearly check-up. He suggested a series of tests when she told him that her heart had been skipping beats and was affecting her breathing. The tests were scheduled for the following week. In the meantime, Dr. Bailey prescribed a medication to regulate her heart rhythm, and told her to slow down her normal activities until the tests were completed.

Gramma agreed to take the medicine, but told him she wasn't sure she knew how to slow down since her body was geared for one speed - fast.

He laughed at her candor and said, "I understand, but give slow a try this week."

Loren remembered that on their last night together they ate soup and salad, washed the dishes and settled down to watch a favorite TV program. Halfway through the program, Gramma claimed she needed her beauty rest and was going to bed early. They stood, and Loren embraced her, holding her close and kissing her soft cheek.

Smoothing Loren's hair with her time-worn hands, Gramma whispered, "Remember, love has no boundaries. It surpasses time and distance, and it is as close as the memory in your heart."

Reluctant to let her go, Loren held her a little while longer, then took her hand and walked with her to her bedroom. At the door, Gramma turned to Loren and caressed her cheek with her soft hand. Loren reached up to cover her hand and drew it close to her lips. "It will be okay, Loren. I love you so very much. Put your trust in God, He will never fail you."

Gramma crossed the room, and Loren watched as she turned back the covers and lay down. She closed the door and waited a moment longer, feeling uneasy. Not knowing what else to do, Loren locked up the house, and even though she felt restless she went to bed.

Sleep was elusive; it was well past midnight when her body finally shut down. After barely closing her eyes, she woke with a sudden jolt. Glancing at the clock she saw it was three a.m.

Something's wrong.

Loren felt paralyzed as she attempted to throw the covers aside and rise from the bed. Her foot caught on the blanket, and she landed with a thud on the floor as her head landed against the side of the bed railing. Stunned by the blow to her head, she laid there, her breath coming out in shallow puffs. Shaking from head to toe, she scrambled frantically to stand. She finally made it to her knees and pulled herself up by holding onto the edge of the bed.

Shaking her head to clear it, she ran down the hallway to Grammas' room. When she opened the door she heard Gramma gasping for breath.

"Oh God help me," she cried as she ran to the bed. "Gramma . . . Gramma . . . answer me please . . . Gramma! There was no response.

Loren turned on the light and saw that her face was tinged a blue color - She touched her neck, desperately feeling for a pulse - there wasn't one and her skin felt clammy and cold.

She was staring at the classic signs of a heart attack and she needed to get help in a hurry. She grabbed the phone, punching in 911. The dispatcher's voice helped to calm her enough that she could let them know what was happening and give directions to her house.

Pacing back and forth by the bed she heard the wail of the siren in less than ten minutes, though it seemed like it took hours. She ran to the door to let them in, and stood helplessly by as the first responders checked for vital signs and prepared Gramma for the ride to Memorial Hospital where Dr. Bailey was waiting.

With the sound of the siren shrieking in the darkness of the pre-dawn sky, Loren changed into jeans and a shirt. She ran a comb through her hair, grabbed a jacket and ran to her car. The hospital was fifteen minutes away;

she made it in less time, parked the car and raced through the Emergency entrance.

"Where is Lillian Hurst? She came in by Rescue,"

"Sit down, Miss. I'll find out for you," the volunteer at the desk said.

Taking the seat nearest the double doors, Loren watched as people came and went through the doors, for what seemed like forever to her. She dropped her head, closed her eyes and sent up pleading prayers to God that he would spare the only parent she had ever known.

A gentle tap on her shoulder caused her to open her eyes and look at the nurse standing in front of her. "Are you with Mrs. Hurst?"

"Yes."

Come with me. The doctor will speak with you now."

She followed the nurse into a small room and turned her back to the door, continuing her desperate prayer. She turned around when Dr. Bailey called her name. He didn't have to say another word - she saw it in his eyes - Gramma was gone.

Taking her hand in his, Dr. Bailey said, "There was nothing I could do, Loren. Her heart just gave out. I am so sorry."

. . .

The dancing pattern of sunlight on the couch caught her attention, returning her thoughts to the present.

It was your time to go, Gramma. You always said, when it's your time, no one can stop it.

Loren remembered she had an appointment with Grammas' lawyer, Abe Cook, at nine o'clock tomorrow. He had pulled her aside at the memorial service to ask her to meet with him concerning a matter that Gramma had asked him to take care of.

She picked up her coat that she had tossed on the chair in the dining room, and started toward the hall closet to hang it up.

She heard a ping as Grammas' keys fell from the pocket to land on the floor. She reached down to get them and noticed a small gold key on the key ring. She had not noticed it when she locked the door at Grammas' house earlier. Staring at it she said, "That's strange. I wonder what it opens?"

Holding it in her hand, she tried to remember if Gramma had ever mentioned what it unlocked. She couldn't recall her talking about it, but she decided she would put it in her purse and show it to Mr. Cook tomorrow.

Maybe he knows what it unlocks.

Three

A restless night left Loren's emotions in shreds. Sleep deprived, she stared at the tiny rays of sunlight peeking through the wooden slats at the bedroom windows.

A memory whispered, causing her to smile. "Sunshine is God's warm caress on a cold world. Wrap yourself in it and it will drive the chills away," Loren said, quoting one of Grammas' favorite home remedies.

You were a wise woman, Gramma. You brought out the best in everyone, even when they had forgotten how.

"Rise and shine, old girl. You've got business to attend to," she chided, as she threw back the covers.

Walking barefoot into the kitchen, she got out cereal and fruit for a quick breakfast. She had gone to the grocery store last night before going to bed, to pick up a few basic items. She would stop later today to stock up after her appointment with Mr. Cook.

Taking her empty bowl to the sink, Loren poured a second cup of coffee and walked to the window facing the gulf. She savored the taste of the coffee with flavored cream.

"It's going to be a good day," she told the sea gulls that were gathered on the sandy beach, squawking with each other.

She stood there watching them argue over a fish that had been thrown aside, perhaps by a fisherman who didn't think it was worth taking home.

"Oh well, one person's loss is another's gain," she said, as she lifted her cup in a silent salute to the winning seagull.

The appointment with the lawyer nagged at her mind. She and Gramma had never discussed her will. Loren supposed they thought they would have more time, but unfortunately time had run out.

Noticing her purse lying on the table, Loren reached in to find the key she had put in there last night. She held it in her hands; it lay there like an omen and she whispered, "Will you bring good or bad into my life?"

Returning the key to her purse, Loren hurried to the shower. While the warm water ran down her body, her mind was considering all the possible explanations about the key; the fact that Gramma had never showed it to her somehow bothered her, making her feel left out. She knew everyone had a right to their privacy, but she and Gramma had always shared the important things in their lives. Apparently, the key was important, or it would not have been on Grammas' key ring. Mulling through the 'what ifs' didn't provide an answer so Loren let it go for the time being.

Dressed in navy-blue slacks, a white silk blouse and a warm jacket, in green and navy checks, Loren finished her makeup and added a trio of bangle bracelets.

With a confident stride in her step, she said good morning to several neighbors who were leaving just as she was.

By the time her car door was unlocked and she slid under the steering wheel, she was glad she had worn a jacket. North Florida had not hit spring yet and the March winds blew cold across the Gulf of Mexico until mid-day.

Loren turned onto Laurel Street and flowed with the early morning traffic toward Main Street. She drove slowly as she approached downtown and admired the white wooden structure of one of Monroe's oldest buildings. The church, with its steeple topped by a silver cross, was beautiful. It still had the original stained-glass windows, depicting the Biblical events in the life of Jesus. The deep crimson, gold and blue colors of the windows glistened in the sunlight. It gave her the peaceful feeling that she needed this morning, as she drove to her meeting with Abe Cook.

The lawyer's office was located in a line of buildings that were also some of the oldest in town. They had been renovated by the Monroe Historical Society as part of their project to restore the town to its former beauty. The project was ongoing. The movers and shakers of the Historical Society continued to secure state grants and hold fund-raisers to gain monies to complete their dream.

Loren smiled when she thought about one of the recent fund-raisers. It was a Donkey Basketball game, where the faculty and teachers at the local schools pitted their athletic skills against the High School Basketball team. It was hilarious, with the students defeating the adults in a resounding victory.

It was truly a town effort, with everyone participating tirelessly to make their town the most desirable place to live in Florida. They were committed, and would not settle for less.

When she'd parked, she had a few minutes to spare. Loren sat in front of Mr. Cook's office, looking west down Main Street. The 1900-Era County Courthouse sat, like a rare gem on a lawn of green in the center of the town square. Completely restored, it was a favorite place for tourist and locals, who stopped to sit in the turn-of-the-century gazebo to visit and snap photographs.

Main Street was ablaze with color, flowers spilling from the stone pots lining the sidewalks. It was a feast for the senses. A feast she and Gramma had enjoyed often, as they walked from Dottie's Treats to the gazebo with triple-dip ice-cream cones in their hands. Loren smiled, as she remembered the way the melting ice-cream would run down their arms to drip off their elbows. They would laugh until their sides would ache at their sticky situation.

I love this town . . . Loren thought, as she walked into the office and said good morning to Ms. Nelle who was the ultimate secretary/receptionist/all-efficient person. She had been a fixture in Mr. Cook's office for as long as Loren could remember.

"Morning," Ms. Nelle said, pushing her half-glasses up on her prominent nose. She was dressed in a dark suit, giving her a proper appearance. Loren always wondered how she maintained her same look, year after year.

She sat, but stood immediately when Mr. Cook opened the door to invite her to join him in his office.

"Morning, Loren," he said with the lilt of the Irish tongue he retained, even though he called America home for the past thirty years. He offered a handshake, returned by Loren and asked her to take a seat.

Quietly reaching in her purse she found the key, and held it in her hand. She needed to hold something that she knew Gramma had held, to draw her presence close to her. A feeling of strength filled Loren, and she was thankful to have this small reminder that connected her to Gramma.

Loren watched as Mr. Cook placed a blue folder on the desk.

She heard the kindness in his voice as he said, "Loren, Lil was a fine Christian lady, a friend to many. You know that she loved you so very much. It was her desire that you have the means to get a good start in life. She set aside the insurance funds that came to you at the death of your parents, never using a single penny to raise you. I invested those funds for her and they have done very well. There is also an additional insurance policy coming from her death. As her only living relative, it all belongs to you."

"There is another matter I need to tell you about," he said, placing a sealed envelope in front of Loren.

"That's Grammas' handwriting," Loren said sitting up straighter.

"Yes it is, but before you read the letter, I need to ask you a question."

He laid a small, gold key on the letter. "Do you have the matching key?"

Before answering, Loren stared at the key he had placed on the envelope. She squeezed the key tightly in her hand. Questions flooded her mind – Lord, do I show him the key?

Peace filled her heart . . . *Trust God, Loren.*

She slowly opened her hand to reveal the key, and carefully laid it on the desk beside his.

"Okay, that's good. I'm going to leave you for a while so that you can read your Grammas' letter. Let me know when you've finished, and we will continue the business she asked me to take care of. The keys hold the answer, Loren. Let me know when you are ready."

Four

Loren drew in a shaky breath. She moved the keys and picked up the letter. Her heart was pounding as she unsealed the envelope. The thought flashed through her mind that the contents of the letter could change her life.

Determined to move forward, she asked God to be with her, to give her the ability to understand His plan for her life. She opened the letter and began to read.

Baby Girl,

I know if you are reading this, I have gone on to be with our Lord. The questions are swirling in your mind. I'll try to answer some of them; others will be answered by the actions you choose to take.

The key you found was never hidden from you. You never noticed it, so I didn't mention it either. Now, you have the key and the day has arrived for you to find out what it unlocks.

You are the child of my heart, you carry the DNA of all those who came before you. Their heritage flows in your veins. One of those is your Great, Great, Great, Great Grandmother Georgiana Walker Collins. The special connection you share is more than genetics, it is a Legend of Promise, and it rightfully belongs to you.

The Legend is destined to come into the hands of the first-born daughter when she reaches her twenty-fifth birthday. It cannot be revealed until that time.

As those did before me, I passed the Legend to my daughter Grace at her twenty-fifth birthday. She, like all of us, embraced what God had entrusted to our family. That is, until three days before her death. She came to my house and told me I must hide it. For a reason she could not explain she knew the Promise was in danger of being discovered by someone who had plans to misuse it. She was agitated, crying. I could not console her. So, to appease her and to ease her pain I hid it.

She died without understanding why she felt so threatened. I never understood either but I know her concern was real. In the years since her death I have been made to feel very uncomfortable, as if someone is watching and waiting. There have been times that I would come home and it would seem that things in our house had been moved around. I cannot explain it, Loren it's just there, waiting to strike again.

After the brutal death of your mother, I secretly took the chest containing the Legend of Promise and locked it away. I chose to erase the blessing entrusted to our family. My grief ruled my heart . . . my daughter was gone . . . I made the Promise go away too.

Perhaps I would have fulfilled my commitment to reveal the Legend to you that should have been your Mama's to fulfill when you reached twenty-five, perhaps not. That is why I wrote this letter, just in case circumstances prevent me from making that decision.

The Legend of Promise came to Georgiana almost two-hundred years ago in one of the darkest times of our Nation. First-born daughters have been faithful to protect it. I failed, Loren. Please forgive me. I was wrong. Our family was given a gift that goes beyond our personal wants and desires - and it goes beyond my sorrow.

This letter is the best I can do to ensure the Legend will not be lost to a world that will someday need its Promise.

The keys will unlock the hiding place known only to me and my trusted friend, Abe Cook. The contents will unlock the Promise for you, our next first-born daughter.

My prayers and love go before you to protect and guide you as you begin the journey that will reveal your heritage. Stay strong and trust God, He will never fail you.

With all my love,

Gramma

. . .

Loren folded the letter, put it in her purse and drew her arms tightly around her body in an effort to control the shaking that spread over her. Her heart was shattered - she was broken - what in the world was she to do with this mystery dumped in her life.

She was twenty-three; did Gramma want her to wait for her twenty-fifth birthday to unlock the secret? Gramma had left her the letter but she could not know that she would die before Loren was old enough to receive the legend.

She sat there; overwhelmed with the direction her life was taking.

She turned to God. She had been taught all of her life that God had a path for each of us to follow, plans to prosper us, never to cause us harm.

"God, the decisions I make today will affect the rest of my life. I want them to be in agreement with the plans You have laid out for me. I thank You."

A soft tap on the door made Loren turn to see Mr. Cook opening the door to ask, "Loren, are you alright?"

"Yes, sir, I'm fine."

She relaxed and unclasped her arms in surrender. What was done could not be undone. She trusted Gramma, and most of all she trusted the God they both served.

Whatever the plan was for her life, she would move forward. It was time to see if her faith was strong enough to accept her life without Gramma by her side. She had her reasons for the path she had chosen; now Loren would pick up those pieces left for her to follow, and see where the road would lead her.

Mr. Cook placed his hand gently on her shoulder, and said, "Good, that's good. Now, are you ready to see what belongs to you?"

Five

Was she ready? Her answer of yes resounded in her heart. She didn't know if the danger Gramma had written about still lurked, or if it had cost her Mama her life. She had been given the choice to turn her back on the legend and walk away, or to use the keys to find out what was there. Her choice was to embrace the family legend. She was ready to take the first step in this new adventure. She would find out what her family had protected for two centuries.

A glimpse of people in hoop-skirts and grey uniforms, and the sound of carriage wheels and exploding ammunition moved across her mind.

Wow where did that come from?

The moment passed, almost as quickly as it had come. Drawing on her inner faith she recognized the peace of God.

Loren answered, "Yes, I'm ready."

Mr. Cook heard the strength in Loren's answer. He patted her shoulder and gave her a big smile. "I'll put this folder away, and you can follow me to First National Bank. The keys we have will unlock the security box Lil has there."

Loren drove slowly down the tree-shaded street, her thoughts swirling like dry leaves in a windstorm. Arriving at the bank, she parked her car and joined Mr. Cook to walk toward the entrance.

"It's been a week of change for you, Loren. This was probably not the way Lil would have chosen for you to learn about your heritage."

"I know, but I'm okay with her decision. I must admit, the discovery has come as a complete surprise, but she apparently had her reasons. Knowing her as I did, she would never do anything to harm me. She spent her life protecting me."

The automatic doors swung open and they entered the bank. They walked to a bank officer and asked to speak with someone about going to the vault to check on their security box. He told them to follow him and the bank clerk would be happy to assist them.

The clerk put in a code, the door opened and they followed her. The vault was lined with large security boxes on each side. Mr. Cook told her the number of the one they needed, and she led them to a security box about the size of a large suitcase, and then walked out of the vault.

Loren stared at the size of the door, with its double lock underneath a brass handle. Her experience with security boxes was limited to the small ones that held personal wills, land deeds and such. These were big enough to hold larger items.

Taking the key from his pocket, Mr. Cook inserted it into the lock. Loren opened her hand where the identical key rested. She had not let it go since she picked it up off his desk. Loren inserted the key directly underneath the other one.

"We must turn them at the same time to trigger the combination."

"Okay," Loren answered.

With their hands on the keys, Mr. Cook instructed, "Turn now." They heard the combination click, and Loren pulled on the handle to open the box.

Mr. Cook stepped back to allow Loren to peer into the shadowed recess of the box. A chest of weathered black leather, with two straps securing the top, was there.

"Do you need help?"

"No sir, I can do this. Thank you."

He took her hand and told her she could call him any time. "My services as the family lawyer are yours now."

"I appreciate your kindness to Gramma and to me."

Loren watched as he left the vault, then she turned to the open security box. She reached in to grasp the sides of the chest and pulled it toward her. Shivers of excitement ran up and down her body, as she placed the chest on a chair near the entrance of the vault. Unbuckling the straps, she opened the chest and gasped at the sight of a delicate, white leather journal, with etchings of tiny flowers bordering the edges, lying atop the most beautiful patchwork quilt she had ever seen.

Her breath lodged in her throat. Struggling to breathe, and with trembling hands, she picked up the

47

journal. She slowly turned the fragile cover to the first page. The name *Georgiana Walker Collins 1861* was written there in feminine cursive handwriting, from an era of the past. She ran her finger across the writing. Warm tears ran down her cheeks as she realized what she held in her hands.

"Dear Lord, this belonged to my Great, Great, Great, Great, Great Grandmother, Georgiana."

Placing the journal on another chair, she reached in the chest to caress the quilt. A tingle of excitement ran through her fingers and up her arm as she continued to stroke the ancient fabric. She felt like she was sucked into a vortex of emotional feelings that she had never felt before. Her heart expanded with a love so deep that it seemed to span the years between her and the Grandmother she had never met. A longing to learn all that she could about her ancestor made her want to devour the words written in the journal. Then, just as abruptly as the storm of emotions arrived, they receded, leaving a soothing peace that spread over her entire being…body, soul and spirit. She knew she was not destined to take this journey alone. She knew without a doubt, she would be accompanied by all the women of her family that had lived and died protecting a legend given to them through the decades for safekeeping.

She sat there quietly, and knew that love would guide her. This belonged to her people, the family that God had placed her in; the past and the present joined hands with her future. She accepted her destiny with open arms.

Loren closed the chest and lifted it, holding it tightly in her arms. This was her future. She didn't have all the answers yet, but she knew she would find them. She served a God that had all the answers. He had brought her to this. He would guide her.

The bank vault became a sanctuary as Loren whispered a prayer of thanksgiving to God for allowing her to be a part of His great plan.

She left the vault, smiled to the clerk, and walked out with a joyful step in her feet that she had not had when she entered the bank less than an hour ago.

Six

Checking the time, Loren saw it was one o'clock. She wouldn't have time to drive home before meeting her friend, Carolyn, for lunch. She had called Loren, as she had driven into town earlier this morning to invite her for a late lunch.

She clicked the remote to open the trunk of her car, and put the chest in there because she didn't want to leave it out in plain sight in the seat of her car. She left the car parked and walked the short distance to the Bar-B-Q Café. She could see her car from the café, so she felt okay about leaving the chest in the trunk.

Carolyn waved through the glass front of the café, motioning for her to come in. It was a favorite place for locals to eat, and was usually filled to capacity every day. The wait until one o'clock was good; the crowds were gone, giving them space to enjoy their food and conversation.

Friends since the first day of kindergarten, they never ran out of things to talk about and loved each other with total honesty. Carolyn and Zac Petty owned Petty Realty, and had been married for a couple of years. He had worked with his parents since he was in his teens. Now that he had his real estate license, his parents had retired leaving him the business.

Leta, their other longtime friend, completed their circle of friendship. She had married Douglas Turner last year. They met at the Capitol in Tallahassee, where they were government negotiators. Their common interest in world peace had drawn them together. Leta worked as a Trade Negotiator, coordinating international trade for the United States. She said the greatest challenge for our world was to develop an economic environment to eradicate poverty.

Doug was one of America's ace ransom negotiators dealing with piracy that threatened international trade. His belief was; *whatever seas you ply, you are not beyond the reach of America's justice. You will be held accountable.*

Leta's move to Tallahassee had broken up their usual activities, but they still got together as often as they could. At five-years-of age, they had promised to be friends forever, and they intended to keep that promise.

Loren sat with Carolyn at a table in the corner. They said hi to their waitress Jane, who took their order; smoked turkey, sweet potato fries and sweet iced tea. Their slice of Key-lime pie would come later.

They watched her go to the kitchen to put their order in before Carolyn looked Loren in the eye and said, "Spill it. What did Mr. Cook tell you?"

In a quandary, Loren squirmed in her seat, as Carolyn never took her eyes off her. On one hand, she wanted to tell her friend everything she had learned that morning, but on the other hand she was duty-bound to keep the legend a secret. The struggle waged inside her. Their friendship was built on honesty, and she had never needed to hide a part of her life from her best friend, until now. Her allegiance to her family won, with her choosing to share the financial benefits Gramma had left her, but she never said a word about Grammas' letter and the Legend of Promise she had inherited.

They enjoyed the delicious food and talked about the possibility of Leta and Doug moving abroad.

"I better go to work. I have two houses to show today. Wish me luck."

They said goodbye, and Loren returned to her car for the drive home. As she drove she thought about the chest resting in the trunk of the car.

What in the world have I fallen into?

Somehow, she imagined she knew the thoughts of Alice in Wonderland when she tumbled into the rabbit hole.

Seven

A stop by the market for food and cleaning supplies took up the better part of an hour. Several friends offered their condolences as Loren made her purchases. It was a good reminder of the caring community she lived in. She decided to drop by the post office to give them her change of address before going home.

With her arms full of grocery bags, she turned as her neighbor, Harry, pulled into the parking space beside her. "Looks like you need an extra pair of arms, Loren."

"Thanks, Harry, I appreciate the offer, but I can carry this."

"Liz and I saw the guys bring your furniture yesterday. She said if I saw you today to invite you over for coffee. She'll be home in about twenty minutes."

"I would love to, Harry, but I need to get my groceries inside. Can I get a rain check?"

"Yes, I'll have Liz call you later."

Loren put her purchases on the kitchen counter and returned to her car to get the chest. Carrying the chest to her bedroom, Loren could hardly wait to open it again. She sat it down on the table at the end of the bed, and opened it.

Her second look at the journal and quilt lying there was as thrilling as the first time. Closing her eyes, she took a deep breath. "Wish you were here to share this moment with me, Gramma." With that thought, she took the letter from her purse that Gramma had written her. She tucked it in the folds of the quilt and said, "We'll do this together, just like old times."

Loren picked up the journal, opened it to read again the name of her Great-Great-Great-Great Grandmother – *Georgiana Walker Collins- 1861*. She turned the page slowly. The fragile paper felt like a wisp of vapor against her fingers. The realization of what she was holding astonished her. She counted the years backward, amazed to find the journal intact with the ink legible enough to read. She held the journal, resisting the temptation to read the last page first to learn the end of the story. Her eyes skimmed the pages and saw the names written there: *Georgiana – Memorie –Marjorie - Lillian – Grace -* it was a list of the names of her Grandmothers, ending with her Mama's name.

Gramma had talked about *The Grandmothers*, but had never gone into detail. The most she had told Loren about them was how much they had loved their families, and what incredibly strong women they had been in difficult times. Loren knew about her Mama's strength from the things Gramma told her, and she knew it about Gramma firsthand, having seen her handle the trying times life had thrown her way. Loren knew it was her time to gather that strength and deposit it in her life in order to leave the same strong legacy.

With anticipation she turned the page, settled against the pillows and began to read.

January 1, 1861
Peron, Georgia

Today is my wedding day. When the church bells chime the noon hour I will marry the man of my dreams, Richard Collins. He has held my heart from the time we became best friends as children. The years passed, and our friendship grew, until we recognized the bond we shared as friends was a love that would last a lifetime.

Daddy and Mama invited the entire town of Peron to celebrate with us. Mama, Alice and I have cooked for days to prepare enough food for all the friends and family who are attending.

I will wear a gown of white satin and lace with a halo of honeysuckle for my hair.

The church is decorated with honeysuckle and magnolias, the two most glorious smells in the entire state of Georgia.

Midnight

I am sitting here gazing at the face of my beloved Richard as he sleeps peacefully. When he took me in his arms, pressed his sweet lips to mine and vowed to love me forever, it was the most amazing moment of my life. Nothing or no one will ever take that moment away.

I pledge to be the one who will complete his life, to love him forever.

. . .

January 9, 1861

I adore the house Richard built last year. His office is within walking distance in Peron. He is the County Surveyor. He said his job is very important to our town as more and more people are settling here.

Our town is a wonderful place to live. Peron was established in 1832. Before then it was part of the Cherokee nation. The courthouse sits in the middle of the town square. Businesses line the area completing the outer square. The Simmons Hotel is a popular stop for weary folks traveling by stagecoach. We can boast about our merchants, lawyers and doctors who chose to settle here. We are a town 'on the move', growing and thriving.

. . .

January 15, 1861

My dear friend Alice comes every day to help me work on the wedding quilt as soon she has completed all her chores at Mama's house.

It is a southern tradition for the women of the community to present a new bride with a quilt on her wedding day, but I had asked mama not to carry out the tradition for me. At twenty-five, and unmarried, some considered me an old-maid.

When Richard declared his love for me, I told the good women of the community I would like to make my own wedding quilt, since I was a late-bloomer.

Alice is helping me quilt the Double-Wedding Ring pattern. We have cut tiny strips and squares and joined them to form a double circle surrounding a solid center. Prints of pinks, yellows, greens, and blues in checks and flowers lay next to the creamy muslin. Most of the fabric is scraps from dresses Mama made for me as a child.

This is a special quilt. I will present it to Richard as a gift of love.

. . .

January 20, 1861

Alice and I continue to piece the quilt. My time is divided between taking care of my home and helping Mama take care of Daddy. In a freak accident last month, he fell from the roof of the barn he was repairing, breaking his leg. The doctor set the leg, but it is not healing properly.

While helping Mama prepare dinner, I overheard a visitor tell Daddy we are headed toward involvement in a war. The talk of a war between the states is on everyone's mind. Their voices are heated as lines of division are drawn among neighbors.

I told Richard about the conversation. We pray the man was wrong.

. . .

January 25, 1861

News arrived today that Georgia seceded from the Union January 19. Nine more states are threatening to follow. Richard has said he will defend our honor, no matter what the cost. I fear the outcome of his declaration.

. . .

Loren laid the journal down as she realized what was on the horizon. *The Civil War* – Oh, *my Lord* – *they were involved in the war!*

The loud ticking from the clock on the nightstand caught her attention. It was getting late. Tired in body, but yet wide awake, she opened to the page held in place by her finger. The growing need to learn more about her ancestors who experienced one of the darkest times in American history brought her eyes back to the written words.

February 10, 1861

I have a secret. Mama Belle came by today and confirmed what I already suspected. I am carrying our first child. When Richard returns home tonight I'll share this marvelous news with him. My heart is already filled with love for the tiny miracle that rests inside my womb.

. . .

February 11, 1861

The smile on Richard's face has not dimmed since I told him last night that we would become parents before Thanksgiving. He grabbed me in his arms, lifting me high as he twirled us around the room. His laughter echoed to the four corners before he set me down on my feet so he could wipe the tears of joy from his face. I have never felt more loved in my life.

March 1, 1861

Daddy has recovered enough that I no longer make the daily trips to their farm. Richard goes to his office each day, but returns home by early afternoon. He says people are afraid to purchase property. The talk of war hangs over everyone's head.

Alice and I continue to work on the quilt. We are hindered by the lack of materials available. Mr. Lucas at the general store told me yesterday the shipments are being delayed from Atlanta. He was told small bands of renegades are stopping the wagons and trains to pilfer. I fear our country is losing sight of what is fair and decent. Richard tells me several southern states have formed the Confederate States of America. I can't imagine what will happen to a country divided among its self.

April 12, 1861

We are at war. Richard came home today with the news that the Confederate troops fired on Fort Sumner in South Carolina. He, along with many of Peron's men will leave within the month to join the fight in the War of Northern Aggression. My heart is broken, but I know I have no choice in the matter. Richard is a man of principle. He will stand with the Confederacy.

. . .

Loren put the journal aside, her mind filled with the heartbreak of the words she had read. She pulled the quilt her grandmother had held in her hands close to two centuries ago, from the chest. Drawing it up the length of her body to her face, she inhaled the fragrance of the fabric before she lay back against the bed, and closed her eyes.

Her last thought, before she fell asleep was – did my grandfather ever return.

Eight

Loren dreamed of a beautiful patchwork quilt in soft pastels, spread across a homemade quilting frame. Hands, one pair white, the other black, held needles, moving the thread with an in and out motion that made a soft, sighing sound, as they worked on the quilt together.

In her vision-like dream, Loren saw the early morning brightness of sunshine, illuminating the room. She knew she had never been in the room, but yet, it seemed so familiar.

Someone knocked at the door in the small room of her dream. Loren turned to catch the words spoken. The soft-rolling vowels of the southern tongue spoke clearly, asking Alice to see who was at the door.

Loren watched a black woman open the door and a gentleman dressed in a parson's coat walked in. He looked out the window then went past Loren, as if she did not exist.

They can't see me, Loren whispered, but I can see them.

Not daring to take so much as a deep breath for fear she would lose them, Loren watched as the gentleman took the hand of the person seated at the quilting frame. "How are you, Georgiana," he said. "I have a story to share, a story you will become a part of, God willing.

"Continue, pastor."

. . .

He began his story: "As I knelt to pray last evening, I beseeched God Almighty to protect this wonderful nation. I cried out to Him for mercy, knowing the loss of life is great as the war rages. I saw a beautiful being in front of me, whose countenance seemed to have a light from within, although the evening darkness was near. His look of innocence and purity arrested my attention. Calmness settled in my heart, and questions fled from my mind.

When he spoke, it sounded like the quiet whisper of the gentle breeze through the trees. He said that God had heard my prayer.

He took my hand, and placed three small seeds there. The warmth from the seeds settled deep into my heart, giving me strength. I opened my hand to see the seeds. When I looked up, he was gone. I believe it was an angel of God.

As I lay upon my bed, all thought of sleep gone, God completed the plan in my heart. Georgiana, you and Alice are part of the plan. You must find a secure resting place for the seeds entrusted into our care. Will you accept God's plan for your life?"

With a nod, she told Pastor Smith, "I accept."

He placed the seeds in her hand, bid them goodbye, and left.

"Alice, go to my bedroom. I know the perfect place of protection. Underneath my bed is my hope chest. My journal is inside it. Bring it to me please."

Looking at Georgiana with love and understanding, Alice nodded her head slightly and went to carry out her request. Within seconds she returned, and handed the journal to Georgiana. Opening the journal to her wedding date, January 1, 1861, she took out a soft white batiste handkerchief, edged with tatted lace. Lifting the handkerchief to her face, she pressed it slightly against her lips, savoring the smell of the honeysuckle fragrance lingering there. She and Alice had made identical handkerchiefs to carry on her wedding day. It was one of their treasured possessions, but now she would say goodbye to hers. It was needed for a higher purpose.

She placed the three seeds, given to her by Pastor Smith, in the center of the handkerchief. She folded it, stitched it closed and laid it inside the quilt between the top and bottom.

"Don't ever forget, Alice. You have the companion to this handkerchief. It is a reminder of what we share."

Alice shook her head and they silently continued to stitch the quilt.

. . .

Awaken by the sound of a car horn outside her window; Loren got up to look outside. Turning away from the window, she could see the journal and quilt resting on her bed.

Sinking down by the bed, Loren's body shook as she held the quilt under her head. Her tears flowed freely as she pressed her face into the quilt. For the first time since she'd had the quilt, she recognized the honeysuckle fragrance that clung to the fabric. It had intensified as it mixed with her tears. She lifted her head, alarmed that her tears would harm the quilt. She stared at the fabric, and was shocked to see that it was dry, as if her tears had never fallen on it.

"God, I don't understand what is happening in my life, but I trust you. I am willing to accept my part of the destiny that has been given to my family. Give me the wisdom to walk with you, and the strength to carry out your will, in Jesus' name, amen."

Hunger pains reminded her she had not eaten since lunch time, so she went to the kitchen and ate a handful of red grapes and some crackers to satisfy her hunger. The desire to continue reading Georgiana's journal pushed everything else from her mind. She let it go unanswered, knowing she needed a night's rest before learning more. The information would keep - she needed to go slowly – to try to understand what she had inherited.

Loren tucked the journal underneath her pillow, laid the quilt on top of her bed. Moments later, as she was whispering her thankful prayers to God, she slipped into dreamless sleep.

Nine

Loren woke refreshed. Tossing the covers aside, it occurred to her that she had enjoyed the best night of sleep in her entire life. She wondered if someone had sneaked into her room during the night to give her a 'vitamin happy' shot.

She lifted the quilt and brought it close to her face rubbing the fabric across her cheek. She thought about all of those who might have slept peacefully with it covering them at night, as it had covered her last night.

Did they wake up refreshed as she had?

Loren folded the quilt carefully and placed it in the chest with Grammas' letter. Pulling the journal from underneath the pillow, she placed it on top of the quilt before closing the chest.

The musical notes of Bach played on her cell phone. Checking the caller ID, Loren answered the call from her friend Leta.

"Hey, Leta-Deta," she drawled.

"Hey, Loren. How are you?"

"I am feeling exceptionally wonderful, thank you."

She waited for her friend to continue the conversation. A moment passed. With a rush of words Leta said, "The government is sending us to Eastern Europe. We received confirmation this morning. It's official. We'll be gone six months."

"Are you okay with this?"

"Yes. We knew it was just a matter of time until we were needed over there. We leave next week."

Leta paused, "I need to ask a huge favor of you. I can't take Jack with us. I don't feel comfortable leaving him with any one he doesn't know . . . so, I need you to house-sit and take care of him while we're gone,"

"Wow, give me a minute to digest this – yes, I'll take care of Jack – I love that old bird. Why not let him come to Monroe, he can move in with me."

Her eyes scanned the room, searching for the ideal spot to set up the large cage that housed the twenty-year-old Indian Ring-neck parrot. He was a Christmas present from Leta's parents when she was four and had been her constant companion. The two were inseparable.

"Loren, I know it sounds selfish, but I'd rather you stay here. Jack is old and he will be missing us. I'm afraid if we send him to your house he would think we were deserting him."

Loren heard the silent plea in her childhood friend's voice. Leta was a long way from the little curly-haired blonde of their childhood. She was a gorgeous woman, with an independent nature and the natural leader of the three friends. Loren knew her friend well enough to know she would never ask a favor unless it was necessary.

"Tell me when to be there."

Leta suggested Loren keep her apartment since Tallahassee was only a two-hour drive from Monroe, that way, she could commute if she decided to have a day or two at the beach.

"Jack's a good old bird. Just fill his food and water trays and he'll probably sleep through the week-end," Leta said with a chuckle.

Ending the conversation with 'love ya', Leta promised to call tomorrow with the time and date for Loren to move in.

Loren glanced toward the bedroom, and saw the chest with Georgiana's journal and quilt inside. A thought slowly formed inside her brain – what if my answer lies in Tallahassee – what if destiny is providing me a reason to be there.

The questions would have to wait to be answered. Breakfast was needed. A call to Carolyn to give her the latest news about their friends was also needed. Loren pushed the questions from her mind, and went to put the coffee on. A good cup of coffee would help start her day off right.

Ten

After she drained the last drop of coffee from her second cup, Loren punched in the number for Carolyn's office.

She picked it up on the third ring with a cheery, "Good morning."

"You must be having a super day," Loren replied.

"I am, and actually, I can give you credit for my wonderful state of mind. As of five minutes ago, the possibility of you being a richer woman increased substantially, thanks to my outstanding selling capability."

"You sold Grammas' house – so fast – wow - I don't know what to say."

"A thank you will do just fine, and you are very welcome, as well."

Carolyn reminded her about Tom Carson, whom she had hired last month. She said he called to ask about a rental in Monroe. He and his family were moving by the end of the week. On impulse, she'd told him about Gramma Lil's house being for sale. She said he agreed to the asking price. A call to his bank provided the funds he needed. The amount would be transferred to Loren's account as soon as the paperwork was completed and signed.

"It was a win-win situation for all parties involved. They will have a beautiful home, furniture included – your bank account will grow – I will make a commission – everyone ends up happy," she concluded.

The silence on Loren's end was noticed by Carolyn.

"Loren, you are happy, right?"

She released the breath she'd held without realizing it and answered, "I'm happy. It just happened so fast."

Carolyn waited. Loren had given her permission to list the house after her Gramma died, but Carolyn felt a stab of guilt that she had not talked to her before closing the deal.

When Loren finally spoke, her words soothed the worry in Carolyn's heart. "It's what Gramma wanted. It reminds me of one of her favorite platitudes. She quoted it to me often. She told me mama eagles would build their nest out of prickly branches with thorns in the highest place they could find. They would line it with soft leaves and bits of vegetation to pad the baby eagles from the thorns. When the babies were old enough to leave the nest, mama eagle pulled the lining out, a little bit each day, allowing the babies to feel the pricks. The day would finally come when the nest was so uncomfortable, the babies would spread their wings and fly. Looks like the last of my padding are pulled out and I need to fly."

"Aw, Loren, that's so sweet. You're strong like the eagle so you'll be able to fly without a bit of trouble."

"You're absolutely right. Now, for my news," Loren continued. "I had an early call from Leta. She and Doug are leaving for the Embassy assignment by the end of

74

the week. She asked me to house-sit and care for Jack while they are gone."

"Well, how exciting. The big city waits. If I wasn't a married woman who enjoys the company of her husband and doesn't like to be away from him, then I'd go too. I can't imagine my life without him. I think it's time to find you a husband," joked Carolyn.

They had discussed this more than once, but Loren had not found her Prince Charming and wasn't about to settle for anything less. She had dated occasionally but had chosen to stay away from the fast and furious crowd in high school. They contended that dating every week-end was the norm. They thought sex before marriage was acceptable, and labeled her as someone strange to hold tightly to her morals.

She wasn't afraid to hold debates on the subject with them, but she knew her true friends were people of like mind, who went to church in an age when Christianity was challenged on all fronts. Her friends didn't bow to pressure where morality was concerned.

The couple of relationships she had in college were based on friendship, and a mutual desire to gain an education in as short a time as possible. They still called for the occasional dinner date, which Loren was glad to accept, but they knew it would never develop into a serious relationship.

"I'd like a husband and plan to meet that special someone. It's all in God's timing. But, for right now, I couldn't say no to Leta about the move to Tallahassee. It feels like the right thing to do. With the savings Gramma left, I can wait until the end of the year to start work. I sense God nudging me to go. I want to follow the feeling and see what happens."

They ended the call with a promise from Loren to go by the office to sign the contract as soon as it was completed. Carolyn had faxed them to Tom, and she would call Loren when she had the signed contract in her office.

Dragging the boxes of dishes and keepsakes she had brought from Grammas' house to the kitchen, Loren used the time to unpack them before going to Carolyn's office.

She believed Leta's suggestion to keep her apartment in Monroe was a good one, so she wanted to get everything not needed in Tallahassee put away before she left. It would be nice to have a place close to the gulf for week-ends and special holidays.

One of those special holidays was Pioneer Week. Loren had attended every single year of her life. It was held the second week in October by the Chamber of Commerce and Historical Society, who worked together to plan the week-long celebration honoring the founding of Monroe.

Folks got into the swing of things by donning old-fashioned attire. It was not unusual to see people dressed in overalls and chambray shirts, walking with people in 1920's flapper dresses and pin-striped baggy suits. A cook-off, featuring all kinds of coastal fare, was enjoyed on the opening day.

The following days were filled with events like soap and candle making, fish spearing, shell art and jewelry making and wood-crafting. A parade, a community picnic, and a concert in the park on Saturday concluded the yearly event. Thousands of tourists joined the locals every year to participate in the community fun.

Loren laughed out loud when she recalled one of the more memorable years from the community event. She was too young to remember, but according to Gramma, the enterprising committee decided to try their hand at moonshine production. When the business was in full-swing, the sheriff came along and shut the still down. Gramma said the good town leaders, and half the community were under the influence, from too much sampling of their product.

While her laundry washed, she made a list of things she needed to take with her to Tallahassee. The list was relatively small, just personal items, and of course, it included Georgiana's chest with the quilt, letter and journal inside.

She went to the bedroom. The chest rested on the table at the foot of her bed. Opening it, she ran her fingers across the quilt and felt the slight tingling sensation she felt each time she came in contact with it. She smiled, knowing it had become a part of her ritual as she passed the chest.

The phone rang. It was Carolyn letting Loren know the contract was at her office and her signature was needed.

"Be there in half an hour."

At three o'clock, Loren opened the door and stepped into the Petty Real Estate Office. The receptionist,

Claire, was hanging the phone up, and when she saw Loren, her face lit up with a smile.

"Carolyn said you would be in today. She's waiting in her office."

Overhearing their exchange of words, Carolyn walked toward Loren, grabbed her in an affectionate hug and said, "Come right on in."

She sat at her desk and placed the paperwork in front of Loren to sign.

"You seem at peace with the decision to sell the house."

"I am. It's what Gramma would want me to do."

They sat a while and talked about her move to Tallahassee. Loren mentioned that her Gramma had left some family keepsakes. She said she wanted to do some research to find out a little more about their origin and value. She was very cautious not to divulge information about the journal, letter and quilt. As if sensing her hesitation, Carolyn held back her questions as well.

The sound of the door opening and Claire's hello to a client brought their visit to a close. "Join us for supper at Red's Sea-Food tonight," Carolyn said.

Loren accepted and a seven o'clock time was agreed upon. She reminded Carolyn that Doug and Leta would be in Monroe at her parents' house for brunch on Tuesday. Their parents were hosting the small get-together for family and friends before they left for their duty at the Embassy.

Driving home, Loren thought about the move to Tallahassee. Leta had promised to stop by her apartment after the brunch, to give her their house key and answer any questions concerning her house/bird-sitting duties.

She went to her bedroom as soon as she let herself into the apartment. The need to make sure the chest sat where she left it was foremost in her mind. She breathed a sigh of relief when she saw it. She didn't need to open the top to see the journal, letter and quilt. It was imprinted on her mind with absolute clarity. She ran her hand across the top of the chest that looked totally at home in her bedroom.

"I don't know where we're going, but wherever it is, we will take this journey together. Tallahassee could be the catalyst that points us in the right direction," she whispered.

Eleven

A buzzing sound in her ear brought Loren awake. Blinking her eyes in an effort to focus, she located the direction of the sound and lay there watching the fat fly batting against the closed window. Too contented to be bothered by the fly's activity, Loren stretched her limbs and muffled several yawns before she made the attempt to crawl out of the comfortable bed.

She could have stayed there all day. "Lazy-bones," she chuckled.

Watching the sun shimmering across the floor, Loren squeezed fresh oranges to make a small pitcher of juice for her breakfast. Placing the pitcher on the kitchen bar, she grabbed the toast that popped from the toaster and slathered it with butter and fig jam. "Yum," she sighed.

The light breakfast was all she needed after the feast at Red's Sea-Food last night. Zac and Carolyn knew she loved Fish and Chips. They wanted to treat her before she left for Tallahassee.

She checked her cell phone and listened to the message from her pastor. He reminded her about the time change putting the service an hour earlier. The second message was from Carolyn thanking her again for allowing her to close the sale of Grammas' house so quickly.

The dishes were washed and her bed was made before she allowed herself the luxury of reading the journal. Gramma had been a real stickler about getting your house in order first thing in the morning. It was a habit hard to break, so Loren made quick work of the chores. As she worked, she mulled over the dream she had after reading the journal for the first time. She knew it was more than an ordinary dream. Perhaps there were clues in the dream.

With her chores completed, she sat in a chair near the window and carefully opened the fragile pages of the journal to the spot she had stopped reading. The morning light was perfect as she drew her feet under her and began to read.

. . .

April 20, 1861

The last week has been one of the saddest times of my life. My beloved Richard left today. He held me close and whispered a promise to return soon. My heart wants to believe him but my mind is having difficulty in seeing an early end to this conflict.

Reports of the battles are sporadic, but they come often enough to make us aware of the great loss of life. Long lines of war-weary troops march through our small community. Many are wounded, their clothing is ragged and the looks on their faces tell of horror beyond speaking.

Alice and I offer what little food we have. It is never enough.

. . .

May 1, 1861

I went to church today. It is our four-month anniversary. Pastor Smith encouraged us to hold onto our faith. With the war raging it is very hard to believe there will be anything left after this conflict is over. There has been no word from Richard since he left. I feel so alone. Friends and family offer comfort but there are no words to comfort the emptiness in my heart.

. . .

May 14, 1861

Families are suffering. The men left in Peron are working day and night to help the women who have farms. Alice and I walked the ten miles to Uncle Riley Nathan's farm today to help Aunt Mary slaughter hogs. Daddy and Mama were there to show us how to hang the pork in the smokehouse. We will stay overnight and help with the sausage making tomorrow.

I am feeling poorly, must be the smell of the raw meat.

. . .

May 21, 1861

There is still no word from my precious Richard who has been gone for a month. Some men stopped at our house today to water their horses. I asked them if they knew Richard Collins. They shook their heads no. My heart grows heavier with sadness.

. . .

June 12, 1861

Pastor Smith came to visit today. He told Alice and me an incredible story. He said an angel brought him three seeds. He asked our help in protecting this God-given gift. He said the angel told him the seeds would be used for healing.

I use natural herbs and plants that God has given us for medicine now, so, I wondered why these seeds were different. But, I didn't question God or my pastor.

After he left we stitched the seeds into the lining of Richard's quilt.

As Alice and I work on the quilt I pretend Richard is sitting beside me. In my mind I tell him about the seeds brought to me for safekeeping. And, I tell him about our child who rests securely inside me. They are both miracles sent to me by God.

. . .

The tears trickled down her cheeks as she laid the journal in her lap to absorb what she had read.

The dream was real – I saw it happen!

She went to get a bottle of water and drank thirstily. Standing at the kitchen window, Loren watched the cars pass on the street below and tried to draw her mind back into the present. She grieved for her distant relative, Georgiana, who missed her husband, but had no way to contact him.

The clock struck the noon hour but Loren wasn't hungry for food. The only hunger she felt was the need to delve deeper into the words written long ago. She picked the journal up and continued to read.

. . .

85

June 20, 1861

A family on their way north told Sheriff Leggett that the western portion of Virginia refuses to join the Confederacy. They have been admitted to the Union and are calling their region West Virginia. Delaware, Kentucky, Maryland and Missouri are also divided in their loyalty, but will not secede from the Union.

Richard has been gone almost three months, I fear for his safety.

. . .

July 14, 1861

Mama Belle, the midwife in Peron came by today to check on me. She assured me the baby was growing even though my appetite is weak. She suggested Alice and I take walks in the afternoon in the hope the exercise will increase my hunger. Alice is the dearest friend anyone could ever hope for. She moved in with me after Richard left and promises to stay until he returns.

There has been no word from him since he left in April.

. . .

October 15, 1861

A soldier brought news today that Richard, the only man I will ever love is dead. He died from a gunshot wound during the Battle of Bull Run in July and was buried near the battle ground. Although I am alive, I feel half dead. I should have known the moment he left me. In the space of a single heartbeat our lives were changed, our future stolen. Alone now, I face the sorrow that he will never know the beautiful miracle of seeing or holding his child.

His quilt was completed before the first frost fell in September. I declared to Mama that I would not sleep under it until I am holding our child in my arms. She turned her sad eyes away from me at my rash words.

. . .

November 1, 1861

The dawn is breaking in glorious colors of pink and yellow over the mountains as I write these words. Shortly after midnight our beautiful daughter was born. She is the image of her father. I named her Memorie Grace Collins.

Totally exhausted, I closed my eyes to sleep. In the tired recesses of my mind, Memories' periwinkle blue eyes stare at me from the folds of her daddy's quilt. I looked up from her perfect face with its tiny rosebud lips to see Richard standing before me, tall and proud in his uniform of gun-metal grey.

Without hesitation I drew the quilt away from his child's swaddled body to show him the miracle he helped to create. I wanted to run to him, to place his child in his arms, but I was afraid if I moved he would disappear. I couldn't bear to have him leave even though I somehow knew his time to be with me would be short.

He joined me then, holding me and Memorie close, caressing us with his hands, comforting us both. Over and over he whispered gentle words of love. The lump in my throat eased as our eyes met and my heart sang with happiness that he was here. I felt as though he was alive. I tried to speak, but he halted my words by placing his hand to my mouth. He brushed the hair from my forehead and kissed me there ever so gently. "Our daughter is beautiful. She will help you know joy again," Richard whispered.

In my dream I wanted to tell Richard that joy had been taken from me on a blood-soaked battlefield hundreds of miles away. One doesn't heal from this kind of pain. And yet I didn't argue with him. I wanted the dream to last and I feared if I questioned him he would leave, and I wanted him to stay with me.

The whimper of my newborn nuzzling against my breast woke me. As she nursed, my eyes searched the corners *of the room for Richard. I knew I would not find him. The moment of sadness passed and I drew strength from his visitation. Strength to turn from our life together that could never be, to the future I held in my arms. At her twenty-fifth birthday I will pass the Legend of Promise into her hands. It is safe, another generation is born.*

. . .

Loren stood. She was shaking from the raw emotion she had just read. She realized the more she learned about her family, and the legend they protected, the more responsible she was to see that it remained safe. She didn't know why the seeds were brought to her family, or what they were to be used for, but they were a precious gift and would not be lost on her watch!

"When I get to Tallahassee, I'll do everything possible to discover what has been left to me," Loren whispered softly, as she held the journal close to her heart.

Twelve

Sunday morning brought clear blue skies and a brisk breeze that blew across the gulf stirring up the whitecaps. Loren watched from her window as Sea Gulls dove deep into the water to catch their breakfast while beach-goers walked along the sandy shore.

Lingering at the window and munching on a Pop-Tart, she felt a pang of loneliness as she remembered the lazy days spent along the water with Gramma.

They had a big striped umbrella they would drag to the shore and sit up as close to the edge of the water as they could without getting wet when the tide came in. With their picnic basket filled with munchies to enjoy later, they would leave the shade of the umbrella to sit on the wet sand and built enormous sand castles.

They knew the castles would be washed away but the time spent together creating something beautiful was worth the loss that would come later.

It was just one of the life-lessons that Gramma had taught her through example. She would remind Loren that life needs to be experienced moment-by-moment by appreciating the time you have together.

Loren knew she would pass the lessons along to her children should she be fortunate enough to have any. She knew it was the simple everyday consistency of feeling valued and loved that she wanted to provide for her future family. Gramma had given her a solid upbringing with a belief in God and a belief in human relationships. It was a value system that didn't deny anyone the dignity of who they were.

"You made such an impact on me Gramma when you were alive. Now, with you gone, those words live in my heart. I know they will carry me through whatever 'moments' life sends my way. Thank you for loving me enough to raise me with morals. It has made me want to be the best person I can be."

She checked the time. She needed to hurry if she wanted to make the early church service.

As she left the church she thought of Pastor Lee's encouraging sermon reminding his parishioners that God was well aware of the path they chose to take in life. He said God would not interfere with our choices but would lovingly challenge us to make right choices for the best outcome.

Loren knew church attendance was something she would encourage her children to continue. Gramma believed church attendance was a good way to refuel your spiritual tank. She said the hymns and sermons were a compass that helped keep us going in the right direction on life's journey.

She laughed at planning children's lives that were not born yet, but realized she would pass down the things she had learned to the next generation just as they had been passed to her from the previous generations.

Aw, the circle of life continues, she thought as she drove the short distance back to her apartment.

The house phone was ringing as she let herself in the door of the apartment.

"Hello", she answered just as she heard the other person hang up. A look at the caller ID showed Carolyn's number. She dialed and Carolyn picked up on the first ring.

"Why didn't you answer your cell phone?"

"Ooops, sorry, I put it on silent during church. Remember, Pastor Lee collects five dollars every time it rings in church."

"Oh, that's right. We couldn't make it this morning. Zac's Dad and Mom needed us to take them to the airport for an early flight. They are visiting his sister in Washington. Anyway, I called to let you know we are spending the afternoon at the beach. I packed a picnic basket. Come with us."

Loren hesitated just long enough for Carolyn to say, "Good. See you in thirty minutes at the pier. Wear your swimsuit. The water is perfect today."

Her laughter was cut off by the dial tone when Carolyn hung up the phone.

Loren stared at the phone in her hand that started beeping when Carolyn broke the connection.

"Thank you. I accept your invitation," said Loren.

A day at the beach was just what she needed before going to Tallahassee to assume her house-sitting duties.

She wasn't surprised at the insight of her friend calling to share the day with her. It seemed that she, Carolyn and Leta operated as one since they were children. Their likes and dislikes were so similar they rarely had a disagreement since they usually wanted to do the same things and go to the same places at the same time. When one would start a sentence, the other two would complete it. It was friendship at its best and she valued them.

Changing into her swimsuit, she grabbed her beach bag that stayed in readiness stocked with a towel, sunglasses, a water bottle and sun screen. Locking the door behind her, she headed to the beach with a happy step and a song in her heart as she looked forward to a day in the sun with her good friends.

. . .

Early on Thursday, Loren checked to make sure she had everything she needed for her trip. She smiled at the abundance of bags and boxes that held all the stuff she deemed necessary for her stay in Tallahassee.

She double-checked to make sure Georgiana's chest was in the back seat before sliding behind the wheel of the car. The sight of the antique chest brought a smile to her lips. The desire to find out more about the quilt had grown daily as she read the journal. The words penned in the journal were taking her on a spectacular journey. It was a journey she wanted to walk slowly. The need to savor her past grew with the turn of each page.

The drive to Tallahassee on U.S. 19 was lovely. Thumping her fingers on the steering-wheel to keep time with the music streaming from the radio, Loren believed this four-lane highway from the shores of the gulf to Tallahassee offered some of the best scenery available in Northwest Florida. Red Cedar, Magnolia, Cabbage Palm and Dogwood intermingled with Slash Pine and Live Oak Trees stretched along both sides of the roadway. The dense undergrowth of Virginia Creeper and Muscatine Grape Vines filtered the sunlight into shadows across the pavement as Loren drove.

Kudzu, a more insidious vine, was winning the battle to take over large areas of the southern woodlands. Introduced to southern farmers as a way to control erosion in the mid 1930's to the 1950's, it had cost farmers needed dollars to combat the pesky vine. It was hardy throughout the seasons and grew wherever the seeds lay, clinging to whatever surface it touched.

Perhaps that was a good analogy for life. Sometimes we admit things into our lives thinking they will be beneficial. Before long, it is evident they are harmful. Like the Kudzu they cling, strangling out the plans God intended for us.

"Now, that will preach," Loren said recalling one of Grammas' favorite lines.

Loren took the Monroe Street exit that ran right in front of Florida's Capitol building. It was a familiar sight. She had visited the capitol on class trips in elementary and high school. The red-striped awnings at the windows of the graceful building gave it character. The shaded lawns were beautiful and well-kept.

It was nearly noon when she pulled into a drive-through to get a burger and fries at a fast-food chain restaurant. She turned onto Thomasville Highway and ten minutes later she drove into Doug and Leta's driveway. Leta had given her the house key at the brunch on Tuesday. They had flown out yesterday and promised to call and let her know they had arrived safely.

She opened the front door and called to Jack. He recognized her voice and called back a wobbly 'helwoe'. Armed with a bag of his favorite treats, Loren went to the sleeping-porch turned into a solarium where his cage held the twenty-something Indian Ring-neck Parrot. "Hey, you old geezer," she teased.

Jack plastered his body to the side of the cage to receive the offered treat. He parroted his appreciation as Loren sat down in a comfortable chair to enjoy the lunch she had picked up earlier. When she finished, she tapped her finger on his cage and told Jack she would return as soon as her things were put away.

Loren had placed her luggage, boxes and the chest in the room she always used when she visited them. Her voice bounced off the walls as she carried on a conversation with Jack who was taking a nap after his mid-day treat.

She always felt at home here. Leta and Doug found the house in Lafayette Park, an older section of the city, shortly after they were married. A boom in house building in the 1930's had provided a wealth of old world charm to residents who loved the luxury of high ceilings and large

96

rooms built in the traditional Cottage Style. The front porch had railing running the entire width of it. The swing and rockers sat in coolness underneath a painted blue ceiling. Hanging pots overflowed with greenery and colorful flowers. She, Carolyn and Leta had spent countless hours swinging on the porch discussing every subject imaginable when the three friends got together. Her friend's husbands, Doug and Zac were happy to watch sports during their gab fest.

Loren loved the room. It was a garden delight with large cabbage rose floral curtains in filmy fabric that waved gently in the wind produced from the ceiling fan. The matching spread and fabric of the slipper chair complimented the pale blue on the walls and soft carpet of the floor. It was a room where Loren had spent many restful nights.

A look in the pantry and refrigerator assured Loren she had enough food supplies to last through the week. She gave the room a high-five in the air in appreciation for Leta's thoughtfulness.

Jack was content on his perch so she decided to join him later in the solarium to do a little research about the quilt. She laid her head back on the cushion of the sofa to enjoy the afternoon sun as her laptop booted up.

Logged on, she took a moment to softly ask for God's guidance.

"God, I don't understand the reason I feel like I need to find out all that I can about this quilt. It's there, deep inside me, needing to be answered. Maybe it's because Mama didn't get to pass it to me or that Gramma kept it a secret. I know that you have the answers. I believe you will direct me to the resources I need to satisfy the questions. Thank You God, You have never failed to be there. My faith rests in you. Amen."

Loren drew a grateful breath and whispered, "Okay, here I go. I'm ready."

She pulled up her favorite search engine and typed in, *Civil War Quilts*. About a dozen hits popped up. She scrolled through without any favorable results and decided to be more specific. Typing in, *Civil War Quilts/Double-Wedding Ring*, she waited until several sites came online with photos. The third one down looked to be an almost identical match to the quilt she'd inherited. Opening it, she read the information about materials used, the scarcity of existing quilts from that time period and how to authenticate the quilt.

A list of people who were qualified to authenticate antiques was mentioned. Loren's eyes scanned the list as her finger scrolled down coming to rest on the name *Dr. Daughtry Corbin, Antiquities; Tallahassee, Florida.*

Her heartbeat sounded in her ears as the rhythm sped up. She noticed her finger still rested on the name and a sparkling beam of sunlight danced across her hand. Peace settled upon her. "That's him. God heard my prayer."

She clicked on his website. A photo of a handsome black man stared back at her. His biography listed the kudos he'd earned in the antiquities field from a myriad array of names of satisfied customers who used his services. A phone number and office hours were listed.

Not wanting to move ahead of God, she left the site up and walked to the window and looked out on the beautiful yard where climbing rose bushes bloomed in abundance spilling over the arbors to run along the wooden privacy fence. Blooms of red, pink, yellow and white blended together to form an outdoor vase of beauty that made Loren want to grab scissors and steal some of the beauty to bring inside with her. Giving into the temptation she found a pair of scissors and went to cut some of the blooms to bring inside. Careful to avoid the thorns, she wrapped paper towels around the stems and decided to collect the mail before going back inside. She opened the mailbox, found it empty, and noticed the Tallahassee Democrat sticking out of the paper box next to the mailbox.

Glancing at the headline, she saw the name Dr. Daughtry Corbin. "Well now, what have we here?" she murmured to herself.

She walked around to the open door at the back of the house and went inside. Laying the roses on the kitchen counter, she looked at the front page of the newspaper. She read the story that told about a recent discovery of centuries old Date Palm seeds found in Israel. The story credited Dr. Corbin as one of the team that had successfully planted the seeds that would produce fruit in the near future. It was all the confirmation she needed. She needed an expert on antique seeds and Dr. Corbin fit the bill to a tee.

Thank You, Jesus. You heard me and you answered.

Loren dialed the number. It rang four times before a professional voice on the answering machine said, "Dr. Corbin is currently away from the office. Please leave your name, number and a short message. He will return your call."

Disappointed but not defeated, Loren left her name and number before adding, "I believe God directed me to find you. I must talk to you as soon as possible."

Thirteen

Loren called Carolyn and Leta to let them know she had arrived safely. Leta asked her to let Mr. Frank, who was their friend down the road, know that she was there. He had promised them that he would keep an eye on her. Loren laughed at Leta, telling her she was being a 'mother hen', but that she would give him a call as soon as she hung up with her.

With all her calls out of the way, she spent most of the night reading the journal. She discovered that Georgiana remained a widow. She became a community leader in her own right when she took over Richard's surveying business. She hired returning soldiers, helping them regain their dignity by giving them a future through honest work.

At the close of the Civil War in 1865 she made it her life's work to rebuild the town of Peron, which had suffered great loss from General Sherman's march through the state of Georgia in November of 1864. Buildings were burned - The Western and Atlantic railroad was destroyed - and homes were leveled by the fires set by Union soldiers. Families who dared to fight back were killed. Farms were confiscated, as foraging troops took horses and equipment, leaving survivors without the means to make a living.

The town rallied under the inspiration of Georgiana Walker Collins. She and the good folks who remained after the devastation of one of the most horrendous wars in all of American history worked tirelessly to bring the Town of Peron back to its former prosperity and beauty.

The next pages of the journal held the entry from Georgiana's daughter, *Memorie Collins Drawdy*. When she reached her twenty-fifth birthday in 1886 the quilt was passed into her hands for safe keeping.

And so it went, from first-born daughter to first-born daughter: *Marjorie Drawdy Gunter - 1909; Lillian Gunter Hurst - 1940; Grace Hurst Taylor - 1963*. Each of them had written an account of the time the quilt came into their possession, how it had impacted their lives, and their commitment to keep it safe. By their own accounts, each of her Grandmothers took the responsibility as a divine gift, and pledged to protect the Promise given to Georgiana.

There wasn't a mention of any one of them worrying about the safety of the quilt until she came to the entry written by her Mama in 1990, shortly before Loren's first birthday. Mama wrote that she had felt threatened by a dread so real that she had made the decision to put the quilt in a safer place than her home. That confirmed what Gramma had written to Loren in her letter. There was someone out there who wanted the quilt. The danger had not surfaced in the twenty-three years of her life, but it didn't mean that it did not exist. She would need to be very careful. If her Mama's death was directly connected to the quilt, and those who desired to have it were still out there, she needed to make sure of each step she took.

It was hers now, and with God's help, she would not fail. Her twenty-fifth birthday wasn't until another year and a half, but fate had placed the quilt in her care before the appointed time. Gramma had taught her *'the ways of the Lord were not the ways of men.'* She would trust in the God who had planned her life. He would see her through this mystery if she stayed committed to Him.

As she read the journal, she learned that the women who had gone before her were women of undying love and unfailing character. Their entries in the journal spoke of hardships and triumphs as they lived out their lives. It also spoke of their thoughts when they read the words passed down by Georgiana – thoughts about the seeds resting in the quilt– thoughts about trying to find out the significance of the seeds. But for some reason, they never pursued their desire to find an answer to their questions. If they did, they chose to keep it a secret.

Excitement shot through Loren. She would find the answers. She wasn't content to hold the quilt in safe-keeping without learning more about its purpose. It was time to see what kind of seeds rested in the quilt.

With the pen held carefully in her hand, she turned the page of the journal and wrote; *Loren Grace Taylor - 2013.*

She stared at her name, wondering if all her ancestors had felt as she did when they had written their names in the journal. The weight of the responsibility that came with writing it there was so real, she imagined she could feel it on her shoulders. But, she was feeling more than responsibility. There was a growing anticipation to find out more about the legend. More than what she had read in the journal.

Come morning, God willing, the search would begin. She would not quit – God would guide her each step of the way – she would unravel the secret held sacred by her family.

As the clock struck the midnight hour, Loren laid the journal on the table by her bed. She tucked the quilt snugly under her chin, and with a peaceful sigh, she fell asleep.

Fourteen

Loren was busy cleaning up the kitchen after breakfast, when the phone rang. Setting aside the dishtowel, she pushed talk on her cell phone.

"Hello, Loren Taylor speaking."

"Ms. Taylor, I am Dr. Daughtry Corbin returning your call."

"Good morning. Thank you for returning my call so quickly, Dr. Corbin."

"Well, I must admit you message caught my attention. How may I be of assistance to you?"

Her quietness caused the doctor to ask, "Ms. Taylor, are you still there?"

Taking a deep breath Loren replied, "Yes, I'm here. A few days ago my Gramma, who raised me, died suddenly. After her death, I was given something that has been in my family since the Civil War. I am researching the items, but I realize I have gone as far as I can without help. I went to God for direction, and my prayers have led me to you. I would like to meet you before I go any further with my story."

"Yes, I understand. I am a believer too. I depend on God's guidance daily. Can you come to my office tomorrow at one o'clock? I am in the Antiquities Research Building. It is behind the Capitol."

Loren agreed to the appointment time and ended the call.

She heard Jack carrying on a conversation as she walked to the sunny room where she left her computer the night before.

"Morning Jack-a-boo," she trilled. Jack answered her with a tilt of his head and something that sounded like, "booooo."

Laughing at the antics of the bird, she informed him he was, "perfect company on this beautiful morning."

With his head still tilted, Jack gave a bird's rendition of the song 'Oh, What a Beautiful Morning'.

Ending the conversation with laughter, Loren booted the computer up and clicked to her 'Favorites,' where she had saved the doctor's web-site. She reread the information on his profile. He had a Ph.D. of Philosophy in History, specializing in antiquities research. As the newspaper story she had read yesterday said, he was credited as having been part of the team involved in the Judean Date Palm Project. Loren continued to read how in 1965 archeologist discovered an ancient earthen jar at the ruins of Herod the Greats' Palace in Masada. The seeds were tested by Carbon 14 Dating, and determined to be over 2,000 years old, from the period of 155 BC – AD 64. They were kept in Jerusalem for forty years. In 2005, three seeds were planted. Eight weeks later, one of the seeds sprouted. In 2008 palm fronds appeared and in 2011 the Date Palm flowered.

Crossbred with its closest living relative, the Hiyani Date Palm from Egypt, the Date Palm, which researchers named Methuselah, is expected to produce fruit in 2022. It will be a new beginning for the Date Palm, whose fruit was used for medicinal purposes in ancient Israel until the forest were destroyed and never seen again after AD 70.

Loren released the breath she held. The drumbeat of her heart slowed. She pictured the three tiny seeds lying dormant in Georgiana's quilt, perhaps waiting to be brought to life at the appointed time, to produce something that would benefit mankind.

Nerves jangling in excitement, she continued to read his web page. It showed he divided his time between field projects, like the Judean Date Palm research, and office hours in Tallahassee.

With no other option than to wait patiently for the appointment tomorrow, Loren spent the rest of the afternoon catching up on household duties. Each time she passed the chest, she paused to stare. She was excited and jittery. There was wonder stirring in her heart at the possibilities held inside the chest.

What in the world do I have?

Shaking off all the unanswered questions, she dialed Carolyn's phone. Talking with her always made her relax, and that was just what Loren needed right now. They chatted about her drive to Tallahassee. They had made the trip numerous times together, and knew the beauty of the peninsular state with its landscape differences.

When they ended their call, a wish formed in her heart to share about her inheritance. She felt empty because she kept a secret for the first time from her friends. Maybe one day she could include them, but, Loren knew that right now was not the time.

Hopefully, the appointment with Dr. Corbin would take her a step closer to finding out why five generations of women in her family had guarded a Double-Wedding Ring Quilt, made of cotton fabric for two centuries.

Loren rested her head against the cushion of the chair and closed her eyes. A hundred times a day, even now, she thought about her Gramma Lil. She missed her so much, and wondered if the pain would always be this intense. Gramma had been her world for as far back as her memories went. Now, her world was changing so quickly that her emotions felt bruised with the impact. She had gone from heart-wrenching sadness to bubbly elation over the past week. The highs and lows of her life made her feel out of touch with reality.

And yet, lulled by the first shadows of sunset turning the brightness of day to a soft grey, Loren knew she would be okay. It would take time. But, time was all she had now.

Closing her eyes, she imagined what would have happened if her Mama had lived. According to Grammas' letter, the quilt would have come into her hands when she turned twenty-five, just as it had to all the women before her. But, fate had changed the natural course of things.

Mama was murdered before Loren was two years old, and her grieving Gramma had locked the quilt away.

'It is what it is' whispered on the air, as she remembered the times Gramma would hold her, letting her know that she was a loved and treasured child of God. Gramma taught her to live by the standard of believing that there is a time and a purpose for all things that come into our lives. She would tell Loren the best thing to do when we didn't understand was to hold on tightly to God's word, and to trust Him no matter what was happening.

"This certainly qualifies as one of those times," Loren said to Jack. She told him goodnight, covered his cage and went to the bedroom. Taking the quilt from the chest, she wrapped herself in its warmth and crawled into bed.

The tingling awareness it brought to her skin filled her heart with joy, and with questions. It seemed impossible that in the depth of her grief, she had found peace. The two words seemed like an oxymoron, seemingly contradictory. Not so, she discovered.

The peaceful feeling lingered, as she prepared the conversation she planned to have with Dr. Corbin tomorrow. Questions deserved answers, even if they'd waited almost two-hundred-years.

Fifteen

"First of all," Loren told Jack the next morning, "I don't want to sound timid when I talk to Dr. Corbin, yes, he's an expert – but, you're right, I have the journal and the quilt. It is my choice whether I want to include him."

Jack blinked his beady eyes at her.

"No offense, Jack, but I need to find some people to talk to. In the meantime, I'm thankful you're here," she said with a grin.

He bobbed his head in agreement, causing Loren to laugh. "Take care, old bird, I shall return."

She grabbed her purse from the sunny room where Jack now snoozed, totally oblivious to the end of the conversation. On her way out, Loren put the journal and the quilt in a large shopping bag and checked to make sure she had Grammas' letter in her purse. She was taking them, just in case she decided to share the whole story with the doctor.

The familiar tingling that occurred whenever she touched Georgiana's quilt, ran up her fingers as she made sure it was well hidden in the bag. She paused and thought about those first encounters with the quilt. The tingling had startled her, but had never frightened her. Now, she welcomed the familiar sensation.

She wasn't sure why she reacted as she did, since the journal had not mentioned any of the previous owners of the quilt having a similar feeling. Perhaps they had experienced the same reaction, but were afraid to put it into words – or perhaps she was the only one to experience the phenomena. She didn't have anything to measure it by. As far as she knew, she was the only one alive who knew about the quilt.

A tremor of fear ran through her.

What if there were others who knew. Maybe that's why Gramma had hidden it.

Her heart raced. She took gulps of air as she told herself to calm down.

I will not let fear rule my heart.

Closing her eyes, Loren said, "You trusted me enough to leave the letter leading me to this legend, Gramma. With God's help, I will not fail your trust. Guide me please, as I learn more about what has been left in my care."

Calm now, Loren started the car and drove from Lafayette Park to downtown Tallahassee. She turned right and parked in the car garage behind the Capitol. A group of tourist nodded and joined her for the elevator ride down to the ground floor. Pulling the shopping bag close to her side, she wondered if one of them brushed against it, would they feel the shock of awareness she always felt. Better not risk it – that would require some tall explaining if it did happen.

The elevator doors opened to a gorgeous courtyard with tall palm trees and planters, filled with red and white hibiscus in full bloom. Loren took a moment to enjoy the beauty. The early afternoon rays of sun touched the faces of the blooms causing them to shimmer.

A register sat in the center of the courtyard, listing the names of the businesses in the two-story building in front of her. She ran her finger down the list and found Dr. Daughtry Corbin's name. His office was on the ground floor, third door to the left.

Her heartbeat quickened, as she approached the door to his office. She pushed the door open and walked in.

She liked the décor of the office. It made a bold statement in black and white. Long settees, in vibrant scarlet red leather, lined the walls on both sides of the room. A black lacquered antique desk that had the look of the French Quarters of early New Orleans sat near the back wall. A beautiful painting of pirate ships, with full sails rocking on stormy seas, was brought to life in bright primary colors of red, blue, yellow and green.

Loren's eyes darted down from the painting when she heard a melodious "Hello."

She held her breath for a full minute, staring at the person seated at the desk who was wearing a billowy white dress. Loren decided she could have been at home in the painting as the captured maiden, fought over and dreamed about by every pirate that sailed the seas. To say her ebony skin and dark liquid eyes were beautiful would not have done her justice. Loren shook her head to clear the fantasy she envisioned, and said hello.

The beautiful person at the desk smiled, showing tiny pearl teeth, lined up in perfection and said, "You're right on time, Loren. I'm Sailor Corbin. My brother is expecting you."

"Oh, my, your name is Sailor – you do belong in the painting," Loren blurted much to her dismay.

Sailor softly laughed. She stood and tapped on the door behind her desk. Loren heard a deep voice say, "Come in" as Sailor opened the door. The tall man who welcomed them stood when they entered the room. Loren noticed the resemblance between the two – he was also beautiful but very masculine, with dark skin and dreamy hazel eyes.

"Hello, Ms. Taylor. I'm pleased to meet you. Be seated"

Loren sat in one of the half dozen chairs that were arranged in a semi-circle. The bold color scheme was carried over from the front office. The vibrant blue on the walls was illuminated by sunlight filtering through large glassed windows. Models of early sailing vessels were scattered throughout the room on tables, and shelves set above the windows.

She sat, and silently waited, until Dr. Corbin and his sister joined her. Confusion wrapped its tentacles around her mind. She desperately wanted to make the right decision, but at this point she wasn't sure what the right decision would be.

A picture of two closed doors formed in her mind. One door led her to hide the quilt like her Gramma had done. The other door would require her to share a legend her family had guarded in secrecy for two centuries.

The enormity of her choices hit her like the rushing wind she had experienced standing on a mountain top. It blew against her slender body, causing her to mentally straighten her back, and press her feet forcefully against the floor, as she teetered on the edge of the moment of indecision.

"Dr. Corbin" – "Ms. Taylor" – they said at the same time. With a chuckle he said, "You go first."

"Okay", Loren said with hesitation. "I told you in our conversation yesterday, that I have what I consider a mystery on my hands. After careful consideration, I believe you could be the person who can help me solve it."

He nodded. "Yes, I am very interested in this mystery. But, before you continue, I want to make sure it's alright to have my sister hear your story as well. She and I work together."

"Oh, that's right. She told me you were her brother. I don't mind, but I need to ask you both for your discretion. From what I've learned in the past days, the objects in my care must be protected from outside sources. I really don't understand the danger, but I trust the ones who left me the instruction that they must be protected. I have made the decision to honor their request, even at the risk of my life if necessary."

Loren sat up straighter, paused and said, "This was literally dropped into my lap without any forewarning. I am the caretaker of something amazing that has been kept safe by my family since 1861. From what I have learned, my family has never failed to protect what was given to them. I can do no less than they did."

She looked into their eyes, measuring their reaction to her words as she waited for her heart to direct her whether she should continue the story or to say . . . *thank you for your time, but I have changed my mind.*

The decision came quickly, without a struggle as she felt the guiding hand of her Gramma gently encouraging her to trust the two people seated with her.

Trusting the inner influence, she knew without a doubt, the time had come to accept the help she desperately needed. She was in safe territory with them. She could bare her soul without the fear of failing her family or putting the legend in danger.

Thankful for the peace that flooded her soul, Loren knew, it was the right time, at the right place, and with the right people. She knew God had intervened and set up a divine appointment.

Dr. Corbin and Sailor sat quietly, leaning slightly forward, and never taking their eyes off Loren, as she opened the shopping bag. She took out the quilt and the journal and placed them on a small table that sat between them.

They remained still as she continued her story; "My Gramma Lil died recently. After her death, our family attorney, Abe Cook, gave me a letter she had written some years ago. The letter told a story about a family legend. A key I had found earlier matched a key held in trust by Mr.

116

Cook. The keys opened my Grammas' security box at the local bank. There was an antique chest in the security box that had belonged to my ancestor, Georgiana, from the Civil War era. These two items were inside the chest. The journal told about certain events in her life; that she had lived in a small community in the foothills of northern Georgia and had married the love of her life in 1861. They had planned to grow old together, but it was not meant to be; she suffered great loss when he died on the battlefield, defending the south during the Civil War."

Loren's eyes overflowed with tears. Her heart always felt the sorrow that Georgiana must have felt when she talked about Richard, and how he was lost to her.

She wiped her eyes. "I'm sorry; this is so fresh in my mind. I've only had the journal for a few days. The more I read, the more I am convinced there is a mission assigned to me. I haven't discovered the mission yet, but I feel it hovering on the edges of my mind, waiting to take on life so that it can be carried out."

Taking a deep breath, Loren continued her story. "Buried in the pages of this journal, is a story of hope. Georgiana called it a *Legend of Promise*."

Loren watched cautiously as Dr. Corbin reached toward the table to touch the quilt. He narrowed his eyes, and immediately drew his hand back. She recognized what happened to him. "Shocking, isn't it!"

"Exactly! Shocking is a good way to describe it. But, I'm not sure why it happened."

"I don't know. From your reaction, I would guess you felt a tingle much like an electric shock, although not painful."

Dr. Corbin said, "Yes, that describes what I felt. Very interesting I would say. I have never come in contact with an object that produces this particular sensation."

Not to be left out of the conversation, Sailor edged closer to Loren and asked, "May I?"

Loren nodded her consent, and Sailor touched the quilt. She smiled. "Well, that was unusual. A real jolt, if you ask me."

Laughter exploded in the quiet room as they looked at each other with something akin to wonder. They started to speak all at once, in excitement.

Loren and Sailor continued to caress the quilt, enjoying the feel of the tingles that vibrated against their fingers. Daughtry drew back as the scientist in him tried to analyze what was happening.

He stood and began to pace. "Well, I can say you are correct in saying you own a mystery, Loren. The next step is finding out how Sailor and I play into your mystery."

Sixteen

They sat facing each other, melded together by the connection they felt with Georgiana's quilt. The peace Loren felt radiated on her face. Even though she knew it was impossible, she felt as if she'd found family.

She saw the same thing in Sailor's face, who had taken her hand. Their clasped hands drew them close physically and emotionally – it was more than friendship – it was a feeling much like Loren had imagined sisters would have shared.

They sat in silence, their eyes following Daughtry, who paced in front of them.

Sorting through his thoughts, he too, was baffled by the instant bond he felt with Loren. From the moment she had walked into his office, he knew he wanted to know her better. He found himself thinking of her like he did with Sailor, as a big brother.

Not finding a sufficient answer to his emotional question, he moved on to the mystery question before him.

Choosing his words carefully, he said, "Loren, I am a man of science, a gatherer of facts. I believe what just happened here is way beyond my level of experience. I have had the privilege to hold some of the rarest objects in the known world in my hands. But, this goes beyond anything I've ever seen. Nevertheless, if you are willing to trust me with your family legend, I believe we will all find the answers we are seeking."

Loren nodded her agreement, and released her breath that she had been holding while he spoke.

"Okay . . . that's good . . . I really would not want to be left out on what I perceive is going to be an outstanding journey," he said, as he took a legal pad from his desk and sat by Loren.

"Let's list the facts, and then we will go over the things we don't have answers for."

"Yes, that will be fine. The known facts are; my great-grandmother, times six, left three items; a quilt, a journal and a black leather chest. I inherited these items at the death of my Gramma Lil less than a week ago. I had no prior knowledge of the items or of the *legend* written in the journal."

Continuing her story, Loren said, "These three family heirlooms are amazing in themselves, but the tale of a hidden treasure (i.e. seeds) inside the quilt that must be protected at all cost, is the area I need your expertise."

She pulled the quilt to her lap and stroked the ancient fabric.

With eyes narrowed in speculation, Daughtry said, "I have a theory; let's see if I am correct."

He held Loren and Sailor's hands and placed them on the quilt. All three felt the effect of the pulsing sensation.

"Point proven – I believe we have a connection based on the quilt."

120

Daughtry rubbed his hand across his chin and said, "There is more going on here than your legend mystery, Loren. We've never met; in fact we didn't have any knowledge of each other until yesterday, when we spoke on the phone. Yet there seems to be a direct connection between the three of us. I wonder if the link is the quilt."

Loren paused before she said, "After the murder of my parents, my Daddy's family chose to walk away from a close relationship with me. All I had was Gramma Lil. Now, with her gone I am the sole survivor of my maternal family line – yet I feel closeness akin to family with the two of you – oh boy, I can't explain it!"

Sailor still held Loren's hand and squeezed it gently, "Same here. It feels like I've met a long-lost sister that I didn't know existed."

Daughtry looked at them with affection and said, "Okay, little sisters, let's see if the journal can provide some answers. You said it chronicles important events in Georgiana's life. Let's take a look at some of those."

Loren told them that Georgiana's hometown, Peron, Georgia, was a beautiful small town nestled in the foothills of the Smokey Mountains. Family and friends lived in peace until the Civil War pitted brother against brother. It was in this horrendous war that Georgiana's husband Richard lost his life at Bull Run.

"According to the journal, the only consolation she had during those dark days was the birth of their daughter, Memorie, and the Double Wedding Ring quilt, she and her

121

friend Alice had completed as a gift for Richard. It is the quilt that I hold in my hands."

Daughtry stopped her, excitement racing across his features, "Did you say Alice? What was her last name?

"Her last name was Walker, just like Georgiana. She was a black girl that lived with them."

"Was she their slave?"

"I suppose some would call her a slave, although Georgiana never did. She was raised by the Walker family. She was found by Georgiana's Daddy. Someone had left her in their barn shortly after her birth."

Daughtry looked at Loren, "Sailor and I also have an ancestor named Alice Walker from the foothills of Georgia. The only clues we have of her were left in a handwritten letter found in a wooden chest, with some of her personal items. It has been passed down through our family. Our Mama has it now at our family home in Louisiana"

Loren and Sailor stood at the same time. Their eyes sparkled in excitement.

Loren asked, "Could this be the same Alice?"

"If it is, then we have just found the connection that links our past together," Daughtry said.

Seventeen

Loren stared at Daughtry, then at Sailor. When she finally spoke, her voice came out in a whisper, "Oh my, do you suppose God brought us together because of the Alice Walker's in our lives?"

"I believe it is very possible. But first, we need to make sure they are one and the same. We have very limited information about our Alice. Tell me about Georgiana's friend and we will see how it compares to our ancestor."

Loren sat and opened the journal to the entry Georgiana had written and began to read about the day Alice was found.

Daddy found a tiny shivering baby during the winter of 1835. It was less than a month after my birth. Daddy said he had gone out on a frosty morning to milk, Old Bessie, the family cow. As he encouraged Bessie to share her milk he said he heard a soft mewing sound coming from the back of the barn. He moved the half-filled milk bucket out of the way of Bessie's hoofs and walked toward the back wall of the barn where hay was stored. He found a newborn wrapped securely in a homespun blanket lying between the hay bales and the wall. He picked up the tiny bundle and took it inside to the warmth of the fireplace. Daddy said Mama came from the kitchen to see what had brought him back inside so quickly.

Mama heard the soft crying of a newborn that was clutched in Daddy's arms. She drew the blanket away from the tiny baby's face and the baby stopped crying. Its round dark eyes looked into Mama's eyes with wisdom beyond her years. 'You're an old soul, aren't you, little one,' Mama crooned as she swayed back and forth. She pulled the nut-brown baby close to her breast and told Georgiana's Daddy they must find the child's mother. It would be improper to keep a black child. Mama's declaration did not keep her from placing the crying newborn in the cradle next to Georgiana who was *sleeping peacefully. She held a 'sugar-tit' in the baby's mouth to feed her until the baby stopped crying, turned toward Georgiana, closed her dark eyes and fell asleep.*

"It seems no one came forward to claim the baby, and Georgiana's Mama had a change of heart. They named her Alice. She grew up on the farm, a constant companion to Georgiana," Loren said.

"She is mentioned several times while they were growing up. She was with Georgiana when she married Richard, and during the birth of their daughter, Memorie. The last time her name was recorded was some years after the War and Restoration. Georgiana wrote that Alice was leaving with Pastor Smith's family, who were moving to Louisiana. She said it broke her heart to see her friend leave, but Alice wanted to see what waited for her outside of Georgia."

Daughtry looked at Sailor, whose eyes glistened with tears.

Without a word, he turned and walked to a small annex area behind French doors. He came back into the room and handed Loren a framed letter, written in small printed script. She stared at the letter and handed it back to him.

Visibly shaken, he hesitated before he spoke. "This is a copy of the letter connecting us to our Alice. It was in a wooden chest, rolled inside a beautiful tatted handkerchief.

We believe it made the journey from Georgia with her when she moved to Louisiana. As you can see, it describes the events in her life almost identically to what you have told us. I believe this is proof that our Alice and your Alice are one and the same. It appears we do share a destiny."

Sailor reached toward Loren and softly squeezed her hand. She and Loren were at a loss for words as they looked deep into each other's eyes for several moments. They reached out to Daughtry, as they stood to take his hands. Seconds, or perhaps minutes, passed as they let the impact of what they had learned settle in their minds.

Daughtry was first to break the silence when he said, "I don't know about the two of you, but I am always amazed by the way God can line up events in our lives. Sailor and I had attempted to find out more about our ancestor, but the letter she wrote failed to give specifics. We knew she was reared in north Georgia, but she didn't name the town. That could have been done to protect her, since many of that day still believed in slavery even though the Emancipation Act had been signed."

Joining the conversation, Sailor added, "Alice didn't have any records recording her birth. We knew her friend was Georgiana Walker, but there is thousands of Georgiana Walkers' in Georgia. We had hit a brick wall in our search until today."

"This is amazing," Loren whispered, remembering the tugging deep inside of her yesterday after seeing his photograph in the newspaper.

She knew she needed to meet Dr. Daughtry Corbin. She assumed she felt so strongly drawn to him because he was an expert in the field of antiquities, especially centuries-old seeds. It had been reason enough for her to schedule an appointment. Now, she understood the purpose of the meeting went beyond the quilt. Events from the past had deemed it necessary for the three of them to meet, in order to carry out a plan that was two centuries in the making.

Sailor shook her head and said, "Yes, I agree Loren. This is truly amazing. It appears the One in control of the universe is at work today, arranging future plans."

She let go of Loren's hand with a final squeeze and said, "Let's have a cup of coffee."

"That's a great idea! I don't know how you all are feeling but my mind is swirling at all the possibilities – at the incredible chance of us meeting. I agree with Sailor. It seems someone other than us is driving our destinies. I believe that someone is our heavenly Father," Loren said.

Daughtry held her hand a moment longer, and said, "You won't get an argument from me – my heart tells me you are right. As a believer in God I know there is no such thing as coincidence. Jeremiah declares God has a plan for each of us. The choice to follow the plan is our decision. I believe we need to follow God and see where this leads."

Sailor went to a small kitchen down the hallway from Daughtrys' office. Minutes later, she returned carrying a wooden tray laden with three cups, condiments and a pot of steaming coffee. Loren took a cup of coffee

127

from Sailor and blew on the hot liquid before taking a satisfying sip of the rich, dark flavor.

Loren set her cup on the low table in front of her. She asked if she could share a little of her upbringing. She told them about the savage murder of her parents and how her Gramma Lil had raised her from the age of one. She said they shared a closeness that grew with every passing year. She told them about the raw hurt she experienced at the unexpected death of her Gramma. Then she told them about the day after Grammas' funeral, when she met with her attorney, Abe Cook.

"I was stunned to find out about a family legend that Gramma had kept secret from me. The legend was mentioned in a hand-written letter from Gramma. She explained the passage of the legend to the first-born daughters when they reached their twenty-fifth birthday. Even though I have not reached that age, I am the sole survivor on my maternal side of the family so naturally the legend belonged to me."

Loren hesitated as she searched her heart, not really doubting God, but hesitate to tell them the entire story. Why would she tell them when she had not told Carolyn and Leta? They were her closest friends and she had always trusted them with all of her secrets.

The difference she realized was that in order to move forward in her search for the truth, she needed their help. She did not have the ability, or the necessary tools to analyze the mystery of the hidden seeds.

With that settled in her mind, she knew the day would come when she could tell Carolyn and Leta everything. But, that day was not now. Her heart hurt because she was keeping a secret from them for the first time, but she knew God was in control and she needed to follow His plan.

Lacing her fingers together in her lap, she drew a breath. Sensing the calming reassurance of Gramma, she imagined she could smell the sweet scent of her favorite rose and honeysuckle perfume. Her decision was made. With God guiding her, she shared her recent findings with the two people sitting across from her.

"Perhaps you will find my story strange, but it's a story I need to tell you because I need your help. I agree with you. There is a connection in our past that links us together. It must be explored, not only for us, but, perhaps, for others as well."

Daughtrys' concerned look held her gaze. "Loren, the story is yours. The decision to tell your story is also yours. I won't ask you to go against what you feel comfortable in doing but I do ask that you allow Sailor and me to be your friends."

"Yes, I would like to be that. I value friendship as one of God's blessings to His children. My two friends, Carolyn and Leta have shown me every day since we entered kindergarten that friends are more valuable to our existence than the most expensive material things. I love the saying that talks about them being, *like silver and gold, their value is untold,*" said Loren.

Believing that she was doing the best thing for all concerned, she began her story: "After reading my Gramma Lil's letter telling me about the legend, Abe Cook and I went to First National Bank to open her security box. Inside the box was a chest. It belonged to my Grandmother Georgiana, whom we have talked about. The quilt and journal were inside the chest. My first contact was exactly as yours; the tingling sensation ran from my fingers and up my arms. As I sat there staring at the quilt, I continued to caress it amazed at the sensation it was causing in my body. It was a definite shock, but not painful. I took the chest home, took out the journal and began to read. The words I read were alive with emotion that touched the deepest part of my heart and soul. The words drew me into a time past, where I felt the pleasure and sorrow of Georgiana's life. I can't explain it any better than that; it was so real, I felt like I was there even though I knew this was not possible. I couldn't put it down, and read well into the night. Finally, when my eyes could no longer focus, I fell asleep with the quilt spread across my body. During the night, I dreamed about a man dressed in a parson's coat bringing three tiny seeds to Georgiana and Alice for safekeeping. In my dream I watched as they secured them in her wedding handkerchief and placed them in the lining of the quilt they were making."

Loren stopped talking to draw a deep breath. The words were churning inside her as she relived the dream. Daughtry and Sailor waited patiently for her to continue her story.

130

"When I awoke, I reached for the quilt, and ran my hands around the center of the fabric. In my dream, I had watched Georgiana place the seeds in the center of the quilt, and I wanted to see if I could feel the seeds inside the lining. Not feeling any difference in the surface of the quilt, I held it up to the light to see if the seeds could be seen. I couldn't see them. I went to the bathroom to get a small pair of cuticle scissors, and carefully snipped each tiny stitch until an opening was made. There it was – just as I'd seen in my dream – a beautiful lace tatted handkerchief, stitched together. Barely able to breathe, and with my heart rapidly beating against my chest, I lifted the delicate handkerchief out of its resting place. With trembling hands I cried out to God to please direct my actions. In my spirit I heard Him say, *Open it – it's your destiny*. The words were not spoken aloud, but I heard them very clearly in my mind. I knew I had to obey – I couldn't come this far without seeing what was there. When I pulled at the stitch holding the handkerchief together, it slipped out of the fabric as if it had never been there. Three tiny seeds lay in the center of the handkerchief. My breath caught in my chest, fluttering against my ribs. I stared at the tiny seeds in my hand. They were three ivory colored seeds, perfectly round. They were smooth to the touch, without ridges or discoloration. Time stood still. I thought about Georgiana holding these same seeds. I whispered her name. *Was it the same for you?* I can't be sure, but it was almost as if I heard her answer with a soft *"yes"* before I placed them back in the handkerchief. My friend Leta, where I am staying, is a master seamstress and keeps a supply of threads in every color and size. I went to the sewing room and found her sewing kit. I brought it back to the bedroom and found a spool of silky thread. It matched the original stitching. I threaded the needle and watched my hands make tiny, even stitches to close the handkerchief and the opening I had made in the center of the quilt. The stitches were a perfect. The incredible thing is – I cannot sew."

Loren leaned forward and said, "This is why I came to you. According to your website, you are an expert on antiquities, particularly ancient seeds. I know what they look like, and I know that I will protect them. But, there is a deep driving need inside of me to find out more about them. I believe God wants us to understand His plan when we are involved with it. He called Abraham his friend and gave him the freedom to talk with Him. I believe we have that freedom too. If we don't understand, God will help us to understand."

Daughtry nodded his agreement. "I understand your concern, Loren. If God calls us to do something, He will give us the knowledge to carry out the mission. I will do all I can to help you learn about your mystery seeds. You have my word. We will take this journey together."

He told her his lab was equipped to handle the rarest and most ancient discoveries. "The method I use to carbon date the quilt will not harm the fabric, or the seeds."

Loren put the journal into the bag with the quilt and held it tightly. She closed her eyes, drained from telling her story.

She opened her eyes when she heard Daughtry say, "We've sat here for hours Loren. I suggest we start fresh tomorrow morning."

Sailor noticed the pallor of Loren's skin and suggested, "It's almost five, let's close up shop and go have supper."

"Yes, thank you, Sailor, that's a wonderful idea," Loren said, as she stood.

"I'll go lock the quilt and journal in my car and meet you at the entrance to the parking garage," Loren said.

They clasped hands, forming a circle. The discoveries they had shared drew them closer to lean towards each other. "You're no longer by yourself Loren. We may not be blood family but the ties we share are strong enough to face whatever is ahead of us – our Grandmothers set the course of this quest in motion. It's up to us to see where it leads us," Daughtry said.

Loren held his gaze. His look reflected a peace that reached out to embrace her. Sailor placed her hand on Loren's shoulder, and they drew strength from each other.

Their choice was made; they couldn't know where they were going if they didn't know where they had come from. They needed to look backward to the past to move forward into the future.

Eighteen

The series of events that had brought them together was very similar to putting a jigsaw puzzle together, Loren thought. As each piece fell into place, the larger picture could be seen. The personal connection between the three of them was mind-boggling.

Daughtry grinned, as if he could read her thoughts. "Well, I must admit I am blown away with the turn of events as well," he said.

"Same here," Sailor added. "But, I hear my stomach complaining about the lack of nutrition. Let's go eat."

Loren left the office to put the quilt in her car. She turned at the door to tell Daughtry and Sailor she would wait at the entrance of the parking garage for them and then she walked out into the afternoon shadows.

Most of the office complex was deserted. She nodded to a couple of girls, as they entered the elevator for the ride to the second floor where she had parked.

She unlocked the car with the key-remote, placed the quilt inside and covered the bag with a blanket she kept there. Her need to keep the quilt out of sight had increased. She anxiously looked around the parking garage and then pressed the remote to lock the car.

By the time she made the ride to the ground floor and walked toward the entrance, Daughtry and Sailor were there. Sailor suggested a café within walking distance.

They chatted about the food and the weather, each of them avoiding talk about what had happened as they joined others walking to the restaurant. Sailor assured Loren she was in for a treat since the restaurant served some of the best food in the city, and the atmosphere was relaxing.

Waiting for the hostess to seat them, Sailor whispered to Loren, "I don't know about you, but I really need to relax. My body is still tingling from the contact of your quilt."

"Me too," Loren whispered back to her.

Over steaming bowls of clam chowder they made plans to resume their research the next day. "My laboratory is located near Crawfordville. It's about a fifteen-minute drive from Tallahassee. I suggest you meet us at the office tomorrow morning about nine and ride with us."

"Sounds good to me," Loren replied. "I've visited Tallahassee many times, but I am not familiar with the surrounding communities."

They walked back to the car garage together and said goodnight. Daughtry said he had an early appointment, but would be clear to leave by eleven o'clock.

"Okay, see you at eleven." Loren said.

Driving home, she marveled at the closeness she felt toward these two who had been strangers until today. She replayed their conversation as she drove past the downtown shops with colorful lights twinkling around mannequins all dressed up in the latest fashions.

Her gaze lingered on the window display of a bridal shop. The bride wore a flowing gown of traditional white.

The transparent veil covered her face that was turned toward the groom, who was decked out in black-tails.

"Wonder if I'll ever be a bride," she voiced to the empty car, as she imagined the age-old dream of herself dressed in bridal white floating down a flower-strewed path toward her bridegroom.

The thunderous sound of a car horn shook her from her daydream.

"Wow, I need to lasso my thoughts before I get run over by city traffic. I miss my small town, with its laid-back ways and lack of rushing vehicles bent on being the first to arrive somewhere."

She turned into the driveway to Leta's house, collected the quilt, got out and locked her car. She unlocked the front door and was welcomed home by Jack's off-key singing.

She paused at his cage and said, "Jack ole boy, I have a tale to share. Since you are the only listener available, have a seat while I tell you a story that borders on the unbelievable, but must be absolutely true."

Jack blinked his eyes and raised the ruff of feathers around his neck in what seemed to be complete understanding, as Loren recounted the meeting that brought Daughtry and Sailor Corbin into her life.

"God does move in mysterious ways," Loren told Jack.

She realized her decision to include Daughtry and Sailor in her life would mean things were going to change very quickly for her. Until today, she was the only living person to know the legend. Now, two others knew of its existence. Two people who apparently were connected, just as she was, even though their ancestor had not passed the legend down to them.

With an expectant smile at Jack she said, "We're going to Dr. Corbin's lab tomorrow in Crawfordville. He will examine Georgiana's quilt, and x-ray the seeds. I am so excited, I could burst!"

"Good-night Jack and thank you for your company," she said, as she covered his cage.

Loren poured a glass of milk. She placed it on a TV tray with a couple of honey graham cookies, clicked on the television in her bedroom and found WCTV, Channel 6 to watch the local news. She dunked her graham cracker into the milk before letting it melt into her mouth in all its gooey goodness. The drone of the newscaster's voice, relating a string of robberies in Tallahassee reminded her to set the house alarm and check the door locks before going to bed.

Bowing her head as she knelt beside the bed, Loren prayed, "Thank You Jesus for bringing people into my life who can help me find the answers I need. I believe if one door in a person's life is closed, another will open. I have been so sad and alone this week. Everything was snatched out of my life before I was ready. I'm still not ready to close the door with Gramma, but that choice has been made without my consent. She's with You now. Please help me to accept what I cannot change. Now, I must walk through this new door in order to follow the plan You have for my life. You promised to never leave me or forsake me. I'm asking You to include Daughtry and Sailor in that promise too. Keep us safe as we follow the path You have chosen for us to walk, in Jesus Name, Amen."

Loren spread the quilt across her, wanting to feel the closeness to her Grandmothers that it embodied. Tossing and turning with anticipation about tomorrow's trip, she couldn't shut her mind down and find a comfortable place to settle. Finally, she fell into a fitful sleep.

. . .

The bright rays of the Florida sun bathed her sleeping form in gold before she opened her eyes to the sound of the alarm clock chiming eight o'clock the next morning.

She lay still, listening to the tweeting of birds as they flitted through the trees, in search of breakfast. She loved the Bible story about how God feeds the birds. It was one of hers and Grammas' favorite passages. She learned to quote it as a child and learned to understand the meaning as she grew older. Gramma didn't uphold laziness but believed we should use the talents God has given each of us to provide for our needs. This belief instilled a solid work ethic in Loren. Of course, Gramma was quick to point out that God owns the world, so everything good that is provided is really from Him.

Thanking God for the solid foundation Gramma had laid in her life, Loren said, "This is going to be a stellar day." She raised her arms in a giant stretch, yawned and

139

shook her body in anticipation for what the day would reveal. She lifted the quilt from the bed, stood up and wrapped it around her body.

She drank in the feel and smell of it, knowing that today when she handed the quilt to Daughtry, there would be no going back. She believed the secret her family had guarded for two centuries would be revealed today.

Loren turned her eyes heavenward, "Okay, God, I'm just like the little birds outside my window. I need You to feed me today. Not with natural food, but with Your wisdom so that I can use this gift You have placed in my life. I promise to use it to help all mankind to understand Your love. Amen."

She stood still, allowing God time to answer. It was the way Gramma had taught her to pray from as far back as memory could take her. It had worked all of her life; she knew it would work today. Gramma called it 'waiting on the Lord.'

The answer came quickly, reassuring her. God's peace flooded her soul, calming her, filling her with renewed strength. It reminded her of the many times she and Gramma had prayed together.

Then, out of nowhere, another memory surfaced. Loren saw a tiny child, less than two, kneeling at the bedside with someone. Loren held her breath!

Mama . . . you were the first one to teach me to pray, she whispered through trembling lips, recognizing the person in her memory from photographs she had seen all of her life.

She let the tears flow for a minute then brushed at the place they had fell on the quilt. The quilt was dry! Just as before, when her tears had fallen on the quilt, there was not a single wet spot.

"Oh my . . . how can this be!" she murmured, as she turned the quilt to get a better look at it. Another thought popped in her head, as she continued to stare at the quilt. She had not even questioned the almost new look of the ancient fabric. Each tiny piece perfectly preserved for centuries, without fading or tearing. She spread it on the bed and examined it from top to bottom. There was not a stain or spot of discoloration on the quilt.

She stared at it in wonder. The quilt looked like it had been pieced together this very day. It was perfect. Her new discovery shook her clear to her toes. Drawing it close, she thought, *what secret will you reveal next?*

Without a clue for this new mystery, Loren laid the quilt on the bed and went to the kitchen. In the past week she had gone from a small-town girl ready to embark on a career, to the recipient of a family legend that was taking her on a quest that she had never imagined before.

She continued to thank God for guidance, as she poured herself a glass of chilled orange juice. She was ravenous and decided to treat herself to blueberry pancakes. With the smell of pancakes wafting up from her plate, she bowed her head and ended her thanksgiving prayer with a resounding amen. The morning with God had restored her, and she was ready to take the next step to find out the secret of the three seeds resting in the center of Georgiana's quilt.

Nineteen

Loren said goodbye to Jack around ten-thirty and stepped out into a glorious Florida morning. The sun was sending slivers through the branches of the Live Oak trees that lined the edge of Leta and Doug's property. She stood still for a minute, looking across the lot, through the mid-morning traffic on Thomasville Road. The road had led her to meet Daughtry and Sailor yesterday. Today it would lead her further into the centuries-old mystery she held in the hands.

She could feel the presence of Georgiana, as she reached into the bag to stroke the quilt. The tingling hummed through her fingers, as her heart realized the connection to Georgiana had grown stronger.

You want to be a part of this too.

The sound of laughter was carried on the wind. Loren's smile widened, and her heart lifted with expectancy, as she accepted what her eyes could not see but knew was true.

Giddy with excitement she said, "Okay, Georgiana, let's do this."

She placed the bag which held the quilt in the seat with her, and drove to Daughtys' office. Cars whizzed by, but Loren barely took notice of them as she thought about the enormity of what she was about to do. She reached over to caress the top of the quilt, needing to feel the closeness of the women in her family. The touch assured her she was not alone.

What did you face when you were the ones in possession of the quilt? Did you do as I did . . . did you open the stitching on the quilt to see the tiny seeds?

The journal had not indicated that any of them had sought to find out more about the seeds resting in the quilt. She knew Georgiana had kept it in plain sight, as she used it to cover baby Memorie from the cold winter nights in North Georgia. When Memorie reached her twenty-fifth birthday she took it to her home, keeping it safe, until it passed through three more generations. It had survived more than seven wars, countless locations with unknown circumstances and yet, it remained like new.

The revelation that she had last night made her wonder at the ability humans have to see things one way, until the light of God's knowledge shows it to be viewed differently. She had looked at the quilt numerous times, since she had lifted it out of the chest, yet she had not noticed the richness of the fabric, or the lack of any blemish. No doubt, others tears had fallen on it many times, yet there was not a trace of them having been there.

As Loren pulled into the parking garage across from Daughtrys' office, she felt at peace with her decision to move forward in the research. She would follow her heart.

There were lots of unanswered questions. One of those questions was why Gramma Lil had the quilt at the time of Loren's Mama's death. Mama should have had it at her house. She must have been so frightened.

For the first time in her life, Loren felt an urge to see the house where her parents had died. She decided she would make a trip to Monroe as soon as she could. She needed to go to the Sheriff's office and see about getting the incident report covering their death. The thought pricked at her that maybe their death might be connected with the family legend.

Oh well, those were questions for another day. She would not worry about the decisions made by those who owned the quilt before her. She was not responsible for their decisions, but she was responsible for her decision, and she had chosen to learn as much as possible about why three tiny seeds had been guarded by her family for nearly two centuries. Now that she had held them in her hand, she would not find closure until she understood.

Loren found a parking space on the ground floor. She grabbed the large shopping bag, which held the quilt, and started across the courtyard to Daughtrys' office. Her anticipation grew as she neared the office door and opened it.

Sailor looked up as Loren walked in. As they locked eyes with each other, she saw the same look of excited trepidation she was experiencing.

"I couldn't sleep last night," Loren said.

"I know the feeling. I didn't sleep either. I kept feeling the tingle I had yesterday when I touched the quilt. I've never seen a photograph of Grandmother Alice, but when I closed my eyes, I pictured the quilt and could see her touching it. I imagined my hands touching hers as she touched the quilt."

Nodding her head, Loren said, "I know what you mean. The connection is so strong. It's as if it pulls you together."

She turned as Daughtry came out of his office to ask if she was ready for the trip to Crawfordville.

"I'm ready."

He told her that he had researched the time period when their Grandmothers were alive. "I pulled up a web page for Peron, Georgia, put out by their local Chamber of Commerce. It looks like a thriving community, although most of the town was destroyed by fire during Sherman's march to the sea. The one building that escaped the flames is the Community Church. The church was built prior to the Civil War, and very likely it is the church where Georgiana and Richard were married."

"Oh, my goodness, I have been so caught up in finding out about the quilt that I completely overlooked the fact that the town may still exist. I want to go there and see it."

"I do too. Maybe we can make the trip together. Go back to our roots, so to speak."

Daughtry put a note on the door saying, 'Be Back Tomorrow' and locked the door.

He said, "First things first, Loren. The quilt is the priority so that's the starting point for us."

"Yes it is. I have so many questions. Why do you think the pastor would ask Georgiana and Alice to keep them safe? If they can be used for a medicine, why didn't they use them during the Civil War, or later? Will they be used during my lifetime? I cannot rest until I find the answer."

"I don't have the answers, but we know that God has brought us together. I believe one of the reasons is to test the seeds for life. We know that anything created by God never dies. It may change locations, but it doesn't die."

"I think you have great faith, Daughtry."

"No, I have faith in a great God. As a scientist, I have seen the times when all of my wisdom failed to provide an answer. I believe God has all the answers to all the questions in the universe. Sometimes He shares His answers with me, and at other times He asks me to trust Him with His silence."

They walked to Daughtrys' long-term parking space on the ground floor. Sailor sat in front with him, and Loren sat in the back with the quilt. He pulled out into the flow of traffic, turned south on US 27 and headed toward Crawfordville. As they rode, Daughtry told Loren about his laboratory. He shared some of the stories when he had worked on different research teams and about their collective discoveries.

He looked in the mirror to catch Loren's eye and said, "I must admit, this particular request for research is the most unusual one I've had."

Loren and Sailor added a big amen to his comment!

They arrived at their destination a little before noon. The lab was tucked into a pretty wooded area, just off the main street through town. It looked like a week-end cabin, covered with brown wooden shakes, red shutters and a red front door. It was sitting among tall oak and pine trees and surrounded on three sides by hedges that were well maintained.

"It's a little cabin in the woods," Loren exclaimed.

Daughtry laughed. "That's the idea."

He pulled the car into a driveway that led to the back of the house. Loren grabbed the quilt out of the bag, draped it over her arm and followed Daughtry and Sailor towards the back door. The walkway was lined with yellow daffodils in full bloom. A pebble path led to a picnic table that sat in an enclosure, tucked underneath huge oak trees.

Daughtry opened the door just as a young woman, who favored him and Sailor was reaching for the doorknob on the inside. She put her hand to her heart in surprise as she said, "You scared the life out of me."

"Well, it serves you right, cousin. You should keep this door locked."

"Loren, the shaking person standing here is Nikki, our cousin and my assistant," Daughtry laughed.

When she said hello to Nikki, she saw a child, about three-years-old, step from behind her. His round eyes were enormous in his pale face. His head was bald and Loren thought his small body showed signs of great suffering. He reached toward the quilt Loren held in her arms. His tiny hand gently touched the fabric as he softly said, "Pretty."

A moment passed, as the adults stared at the small child. Nikki dropped to her knees and said, "This is my son, Grayson. I'm in shock. He is usually very shy."

Loren knelt down in front of Grayson with the quilt between them. She reached toward him, and he placed his hand in hers. They caressed the quilt together. A smile spread across the child's face and Loren's heart melted with tenderness.

As they continued to trace the pattern of the fabric together, Loren heard Nikki say that Grayson wasn't having a good day, so she had not left him with the sitter. She told Daughtry she would put him down for a nap and meet them in the lab.

Nikki picked Grayson up, and he waved his tiny hand at Loren as they left the room. She stood and watched as the door was closed.

Sailor cleared her throat before she said, "Grayson has leukemia, and doctors don't give them an encouraging outcome. Maybe three months is all they'll say."

The silence hung heavy in the air until Daughtrys' fingers gave a short drum roll on the table where he'd placed his briefcase. "Okay, let's go to the lab and see what we can discover."

Loren followed them, praying for the child and his brave Mama, who faced such a heartbreaking future. Her words pled in silent desperation, "Jesus, heal this beautiful little boy."

Daughtry unlocked the door to a large room filled with sophisticated looking equipment much like you would see in an x-ray room of a large hospital. She took a deep breath and handed the quilt to Daughtry. He placed the quilt on a metal table, under a large, hooded piece of equipment that had a mirrored apparatus pointed downward. He explained the procedure in terms she could understand; basically telling her he would take ultra-violet photographs of the center of the quilt, where she said the seeds rested.

He motioned for her to follow him to an alcove where Sailor was putting information into a computer. "Sailor is uploading all the data we know about the seeds. The machine will photograph them and compare its diagnosis with what we have told it. Then it will retrieve any new finding and download it to us."

Sailor pushed the start button, and for the next ten minutes, the machine moved back and forth as it snapped photographs from several different angles.

They walked back to the table where the quilt lay. Each of them automatically began to stroke the quilt, as they waited for the computer to analyze its findings.

Nikki tapped on the door, pushing it open to say, "Sorry to interrupt, Daughtry, but you have an urgent phone call."

"We're done. Come on in."

She came into the room carrying Grayson, who was wide awake in her arms. She handed the phone to Daughtry. He took it and went to a small office at the back of the room. She stood in front of Sailor and Loren, after putting Grayson down in a chair near the table.

"He wouldn't take a nap. He said he wanted to see the 'pretty blankie' again."

Sailor said, "I told Loren about Grayson. I hope that was alright with you."

Nikki shook her head yes, and told them he had an appointment tomorrow at Tallahassee Memorial Hospital. She said she dreaded it, because they would need to get several blood samples to determine further treatment.

"I die a little every time they poke holes in his body, but I have no other choice but to allow it. I'm always hoping they'll walk out and say it's all been a bad mistake. That he doesn't have leukemia. That he is not going to die."

"Mama, Mama, look at my hands!"

They all three turned as one, to look at Grayson, who was rubbing the quilt and then looking at his upturned hands – tiny pale hands that suddenly sparkled with the healthy color of life!

Twenty

"What in the world," Nikki shouted as she ran to scoop Grayson up. She grabbed his tiny hands to examine them, only to discover the sparkle was gone.

She looked back at Loren and Sailor, who were standing motionless, with stunned looks on their faces. They looked at each other, and Loren's voice finally came out in a squeaky sound. "Oh my goodness, did you all see what I think I saw!"

"Uh, well, maybe," Sailor sputtered. "It depends on what you saw."

Their conversation was interrupted when they looked over at Nikki, who was still holding Grayson. She had sunk into the chair, as if all her strength had left her body. Grayson was struggling to get down, but Nikki continued to pin his body close to her.

"Mama, let go, you're squeezing me," he whispered.

Dazed, she released her hold on him and watched him push off her lap to stand in front of her. She stared at him, realizing he looked different, but she was unable to pinpoint the difference. As she sat there continuing to stare at her son, he turned to look at Sailor and Loren. What they saw caused them to gasp in wonder!

"Nikki, look at his face, his skin is pink, all the paleness is gone," Sailor whispered in awe.

"What did you say?"

"Turn Grayson around and look at him, Nikki."

Nikki gently put her hands on Grayson's shoulders and turned him to face her. A smile of pure bliss spread across her face, as tears coursed down her cheeks.

"Dear God in heaven, look at him," she shouted! She jumped from the chair and grabbed Grayson, lifting him in the air to dance around the room. The sound of their joyous laughter echoed around the room.

Daughtry walked into the room to ask what in the world all the commotion was. He looked at Grayson, who was grinning at the adults in the room, who had finally stopped their spontaneous dancing.

"Will someone let me in on what is happening, or are you all going to continue to stand there laughing?"

"Well, we're not exactly sure what happened. Grayson told us his hands were sparkling as he was rubbing the quilt, so we looked over at him and....I'm don't know what happened . . . but . . . well . . . look at him," Loren trilled in excitement.

Grayson managed to escape Nikki's hold, and walked back to the quilt. He rubbed both small hands on the quilt, and then turned them over to see the sparkles again. Loren, Daughtry, Sailor and Nikki watched him. Each time he caressed the quilt; the sparkles danced across his palms, and would then disappear.

Deciding to take the scientific approach, even though he was seeing something that defied science, Daughtry said, "okay, let's take a deep breath and everybody sit down. There must be a valid reason for all this."

Grayson had tired of the 'sparkle game' and sat on the floor, looking back and forth at the faces of the adults who were all talking at one time. To him, it sounded like the noise of the cars and trucks zooming by as his Mama drove them to the hospital.

As they continued to talk over each other, Daughtry held up his hand to silence them. "Nikki, you go first."

"Well, we were talking about Grayson's appointment at the hospital when he said his hands were sparkling. We looked, and for a moment, they were. Then the paleness left him and his skin turned pink and . . . Oh, God, please let it be real," she said, as fresh tears coursed down her cheeks.

As each one tried to answer Daughtrys' inquiry about what had occurred, Loren thought about her overall feeling of well-being that she had enjoyed since her first encounter with the quilt. She had not seen the sparkles, but had felt tingles. She had accepted it without really putting a specific label on it, but now she wondered if the seeds were somehow connected. She certainly didn't have a scientific mind, but perhaps the ultra-violet rays used in the photographing process had somehow triggered a reaction from the seeds . . . *crazy thoughts!*

Have faith in God, Loren.

God reminded her that He created everything, and that everything was His to use to show the Glory of the Lord. Loren knew the Bible spoke about Jesus being the

155

seeds of life that were sowed and brought a harvest of souls. He was still doing that today. She thought about aspirin. It was created from the bark of the Willow tree. In fact, most medicines were produced from the herbs and plants of the earth. But, could it be possible that it was time for the healing in these seeds to be discovered, and that she would be the one to have that privilege!

Trust Me!

"I know what happened, God healed him."

She watched their faces and saw the moment the truth dawned in their spirits.

"Is it really possible?" Nikki asked. "I've heard about miracles. I've read about them in the Bible too, but I never dreamed God would do this for me," she cried as she kissed Grayson's little bald head. She held her child close to her and gave way to the tears. They stared at each other, enjoying the wonder of the moment, holding onto it, not wanting it to end.

"Loren, you are at another crossroad. Nikki doesn't know the legend. It is up to you to share or not. Hers and Grayson's connection comes through Alice just as ours does," Daughtry said.

She glanced at the child resting against his Mama's breast. He looked totally at peace. She could not deny what had happened. God had shown them a miracle. He was in control.

Taking a deep breath, Loren told Nikki what had come about in her life in the past month. How Gramma had died leaving her with a family legend she knew nothing about, how she had been drawn to show the quilt to Daughtry and then discovering the connection between them.

"Now, I meet you and Grayson, who also share a connection by being related to Sailor and Daughtry. I don't know all the answers, but I believe there is a blessing connected to this quilt because it is protecting a God-given Promise, and when Grayson touched it God honored the blessing to touch him."

While Loren told her story, Daughtry and Sailor had listened quietly. Clearing his throat, Daughtry said, "I had something happen to me as well last night. After what has happened to Grayson, I'm convinced there is a valid reason about what I experienced too. I have been struggling with a situation concerning a decision to move forward in an area of research. I haven't been able to solve the missing piece of the find...until last night. At about three a.m. I awoke suddenly, and literally, saw the answer illuminated on my bedroom wall, as if someone had written it there. I believe my contact with the quilt yesterday could have triggered this too."

Sailor rubbed her hand across her eyes and said, "Me too . . . I mean . . . I feel like my soul is being nourished. Like there is new purpose in my life. Crazy . . . maybe, but it's how I feel."

They drew closer, reaching out to each other to clasp hands. What had begun as one had grown to a circle of three, and had now expanded to include two more. They bowed their heads and quietly gave thanks to God.

"I don't have all the answers, but I can't deny what I see. Grayson's appointment is tomorrow. I believe, with all my heart, the leukemia will be gone," Nikki said.

When she looked back at her child, he had fallen asleep in her lap. His little pink hands were tucked together under his chin as if he too was praying a prayer of thankfulness to God for his restored health.

The picture of the resting child lingered in their minds as they said goodbye to Nikki. She promised to call as soon as the morning appointment was over. Hugs were exchanged quietly, since they didn't want to disturb Grayson. Nikki whispered a final goodbye as they slipped out the door to return to Tallahassee.

Twenty-One

The car was filled with excited chatter, on the short ride back to Tallahassee. Loren kept reaching over to stroke the quilt. She and Sailor were literally bouncing with anticipation, as they talked about Grayson's doctor appointment at the hospital tomorrow.

"I wish Nikki would go right now!" Sailor said.

"Me too. I would like to be in the room, to see the faces of the doctors as they try to explain this turn of events," Loren giggled in agreement.

Their talk turned to the possible finding of the seeds. Before leaving the lab, they cautioned Nikki about keeping the quilt, and the legend a secret. They talked about the possibility of Grayson telling the doctor, but felt like most doctors would dismiss the tale as the active imagination of a three-year-old.

Nikki had worried about what she would tell the doctors if they questioned her about Grayson's story. Daughtry had suggested, she shrug it off as the fantasy tale of a child.

"God help me. I can't lie, not after what God has done for us," Nikki had cried.

Loren had assured her God would provide an answer, since He had protected the seeds for two centuries.

Amidst all the wonder about Grayson, Daughtry decided to take the information with him on a flash drive. He said he wanted to look at the data they had from today.

"I'll take Sailor home, and come back to look at the printout from the carbon dating on the seeds while I'm there."

When they reached the parking garage, Daughtry pulled into a space near Loren's car. They sat a minute, savoring the day. Sailor was first to break the silence when she quipped, "We forgot to eat!"

"Yes we did, but I don't feel hungry. I must be too excited to eat," Loren said.

She gathered her things, as Daughtry told her he would call her as soon as he learned more about the seeds.

Loren took a few steps towards her car, and then turned to look at Daughtry and Sailor, who were standing by their car.

"Is this a dream? If it is, it is the strangest dream I've ever had, and I hope I never wake up. I never want to forget seeing Grayson go from a pale weak child, to a little boy with rosy cheeks, and full of life."

"It's not a dream, Loren. I deal with reality every day. This is real," Daughtry reassured her.

They said goodnight and went their separate ways.

Driving home, Loren was surrounded with a mellow glow as she replayed the day in her mind. By the time she pulled into the driveway, her empty stomach growled, and her thoughts turned to a supper of grits, bacon and scrambled eggs. She unlocked the door, and called a

160

greeting to Jack. She took the quilt and journal to the bedroom, and then went straight to the kitchen to prepare the delicious food her mind had conjured up.

As she settled in for the night, she took the journal to bed with her. She smoothed the quilt, laying it at the foot of the bed. The tingling awareness had increased since Grayson's encounter with it today. Loren imagined it pulsed with life, like the bright beacon of light from a lighthouse, piercing the darkness of night.

Opening the journal, she began to write underneath the entry of her name.

. . .

March 15, 2013

I saw a miracle today. Death had decided to take a little boy named Grayson, but God intervened through your quilt Georgiana. My logic was at war with my faith, but faith won. I cannot deny the truth that I saw.

When Grayson touched the quilt, sparkles appeared on his tiny hands. His skin went from the paleness of sickness, to the rosy color of good health.

His Mama will take him to the doctor tomorrow. The appointment will confirm the truth, I believe in my heart.

161

God used our Promise to provide healing for Grayson.

I wish I had the answer to my question about whether all of you Grandmothers, who owned the quilt before me ever encountered miracles too. If you did, you chose to remain silent about them. Perhaps it never happened, when it was yours.

I'll never know, but I must write what is in my heart. I believe there is healing provided by the seeds; that all of you have kept safe. I don't understand how it is possible, but I cannot deny what I saw today.

Should there be another generation to pass the quilt to, I believe it is my duty and my honor, to record the things that have happened. The dream I had the night I first held the quilt told about 'a fulfillment of time'. Is it possible, that time has come?

From the first moment I touched your quilt, Georgiana, it caused a stir in *my emotions, causing my hands and body to tingle as if, I had come in contact with a living thing. Could the reaction be part of the plan to connect me with the commission that was given to you two centuries ago? I feel what you must have felt on that day when Pastor Smith brought the seeds to you. Just as you and all the Grandmothers were faithful to carry the plan forward, I am committed to do my part to see it is kept safe.*

I embrace the journey with renewed hope, from what my eyes saw today. If God used the seeds for the healing of one child, He will surely use them again. I am so humbled by the fact that I was chosen to be part of His divine plan.

Loren Grace Taylor

. . .

Peace flooded her soul as she closed the journal, and slipped it under her pillow. She reached for the quilt, pulling it close to her chin to inhale the fragrance that was becoming so familiar to her. It enveloped her body, and she drifted into sleep.

Loren tossed as the dream carried her farther into the dark woods. She could hear her breath escaping, in gulping sounds of desperation. Low hanging branches grabbed at her hair, snaring her, holding her to the ground, as the footsteps of her pursuer drew closer. Looking over her shoulder, the moon shot from behind a cloud, to outline the shadow of the man who wanted to harm her. She began to run faster . . . faster . . . as she clutched the quilt in her arms.

The tiny pinpoint of light in front of her drew her. It was safety . . . she had to keep the quilt safe. She knew in her heart there was an enemy who had discovered her family secret. She ran faster . . . faster toward the light . . . she stumbled and was falling . . . falling . . . falling . . . as the steps of her pursuer came closer and closer.

. . .

The cold chills, and sounds of someone moaning woke Loren. She cried out in protest, throwing her arms in front of her face, in an effort to break her fall.

Not quiet awake, she sat up in the bed, gasping for air, as she tried to pull herself out of the desperate dream. She turned on the lamp by her bed, and reached for the quilt, which had slipped to the floor as her night of terror raged. Bundling it under her chin, she released the tears that rushed from her wounded soul. She cried until the fountain of sorrow ran dry, leaving her with dry hiccups in its aftermath.

Puzzled by the intensity of the dream, Loren lay back against the headboard of the bed, willing her breathing to slow, and her mind to settle. As she stroked the folds of the quilt, she cried out to God, asking Him to erase fear, and to give her the sound mind promised in His Word.

Calmer, she was aware of the presence of someone gently soothing her troubled spirit. As she sat there, she sensed a gentle hand against her hair. It lightly touched her tousled hair and reminded Loren of the many times Gramma had ran her hand down the length of her hair, letting her know that whatever the problem was, they would face it together. But, there was something different about the feel of this hand. The touch was protective like her Gramma, but yet, it felt younger. She closed her eyes, content to allow the peaceful feeling to continue.

Her eyes popped open. From deep inside, a memory of slender hands touching her hair surfaced. "Oh, Mama . . . Mama," Loren whispered. She knew it wasn't possible for her to be there, but somehow the memory of her Mama had managed to come at a time that she needed her. Memories were powerful. The touch...the smell, it seemed so real. Love was truly a lasting force. Once it was felt, it could never be forgotten.

Lying in the stillness, she remembered the terror in her dream. The darkness surrounding her was so evil, she could feel it overtaking her, as she ran for her life. She had pushed with all her might to reach the pinpoint of light that would save her from the unspeakable danger.

The peace God had sent as she woke, soothed her frightened spirit. Amazingly, it had come with the memory of her Mama. To Loren, she was a beautiful, smiling woman in a photograph. But after the nightmare, she had seemed so real, more than a photograph of paper and ink from long ago.

If she had this memory of Mama, perhaps there were other memories of her. She sat quietly, praying that God would allow her to remember other times she might have felt her Mama's guiding hands. She was thrilled to find there were several. Like the day she had turned twelve years old. It was the first time Gramma had allowed her to go to the movie theater with a group of her friends. After the movie was over, her friends had left her waiting outside for Gramma. She had noticed a man standing near the trees. She thought he was waiting on someone. She kept her eyes on him as she had walked toward the trees and sat on the bench near the sidewalk. All of a sudden, she had shuddered in fear, then she'd felt gentle hands on her shoulders, urging her to get up quickly, and return to the lighted theater. The feeling was so urgent; she had walked back to the front of the theater to wait. Was it possible her Mama knew that she was facing danger, and her protective Mother's love had spanned the years to reach out to Loren?

A floodgate opened inside of Loren. Memories tumbled one on top of the other – when she was three years old and having scary nightmares – at sixteen, when her date was pushing her to drink alcohol – at nineteen, when she was overwhelmed with school work.

"Oh, Mama, I didn't realize it was you. You've been there all of my life but I didn't recognize it until now."

166

She dried her tears. Still caught up in the memories she waited, wanting to hold onto the scraps of memories she was feeling. Gramma had always told her that love didn't have the limits of time and distance. According to her, nothing can separate us from the love of God, not even death. Was it possible that a mother's love could span the separation too, if it remained in our hearts and our memories?

Tossing the covers aside, Loren went to the kitchen to brew coffee. A strong cup of coffee was what she needed to clear her mind. She poured a cup, left it black and walked to the solarium. Jack was silent under the covered cage. She left the cover in place, needing the quietness to sort through the past few hours.

Taking a sip of the hot liquid, she mulled the dream over in her mind. Not one to have nightmares since childhood, Loren knew there was a reason that it had happened. She picked at the dream, taking it apart piece by piece. Then she remembered the feeling of safety, in the early dawn when she sensed the protecting presence of her Mama. Remembering that Mama had always come to her at times of trouble, she wondered if it was the reason she had come now. Maybe she was warning her that the quilt was in danger.

Loren's skin crawled. Cold chills ran up her body! Oh God in heaven . . . there was an enemy out there who wanted the quilt for the wrong reason! She had to find a way to protect the Legend of Promise!

Twenty-Two

Across town, Daughtry sat hunched over his desk, looking at the computer screen in awe. He'd seen all manner of seeds in his years of research, but the three seeds on the screen in front of him, defied anything he had ever seen before.

He knew the average seed is much like an embryo. It has two points of growth, the stem and the root. A seed can lay dormant for centuries, but with the right elements, it can live again, when the roots are fed nutrients, and the stem is provided the right environment.

The seeds he was looking at contained three distinct parts in each one. The inner core was wrapped in a substance he'd never seen. It was a clear fluid that sparkled and pulsed with life.

Daughtry leaned back in his chair and ran a hand through his hair. He stared at the ceiling, and then looked back at the screen. It was still there. The three seeds, containing three parts in one outer part were very much alive, without nutrients, water or sunlight.

"God, I need some help here. I don't understand. This is impossible!"

His scientific mind battled with the spiritual part of his mind. He had studied the miracle of nature numerous times. He believed there were steps to reproduction that when followed produced the desired results. This time was different. According to Loren the seeds had been shielded from all the elements necessary to produce life. Yet, they were alive!

He paced. He returned to the screen and saw they were still there. "Okay, God, let's walk through this. I need to understand what I am looking at. I know that you made seeds, to produce trees and plants. But what in the world are these seeds used for?"

There is life in the seeds!

Daughtry stopped pacing! He grabbed Alice's framed letter that he had shown to Loren yesterday, and stared at the words at the bottom of the page.

There is life in the seeds.

Shaken by what he was thinking, Daughtry whispered, "God in heaven is it possible! Is there healing in these seeds?

He thought about the Presence of God that rested in the Ark of the Covenant, and how the Presence of God led His people with a cloud by day and fire at night. It was a fact, people were healed every day, and miracles were all around us. But, seeds . . . would God use seeds?

The questions tumbled one on top of the other. He didn't have an answer for even one of them. But, one thing he knew for sure. If this was what the seeds were, then he was on the brink of the most important discovery he had ever made . . . and, if it was true, what in the world would Loren do with them!

He checked the time. It was almost three a.m. He had to call Loren. She needed to see this. He picked up his cell to call – then stopped after he punched in the first two numbers – cell calls could be traced! Reaching across his desk to the land line phone, he dialed Sailor's home phone. It rang once, twice, three times – no answer. "Come on Sailor, pick up the phone," he muttered in frustration. Finally, on the fourth ring, her sleepy hello sounded in the silence.

"Sailor, listen. Get dressed; we need to go see Loren!"

"What are you talking about? It's the middle of the night. Why can't it wait till morning?"

"Just get dressed. I don't want to answer these questions over the phone. I'll be there as soon as I can. Be looking for me. Meet me at the car."

Sailor heard the click of the phone as he disconnected. She stared at it, debating whether to call him back. Whatever had him in a tizzy had to be major. She knew her brother, knew he wasn't given to panic, but panic was what she'd heard in his voice. Sailor yawned, and shook off the remaining sleepiness before she went to get dressed. Daughtry said to meet him at the car, and she planned to do just that. She wanted to see what had her brother so up in the air.

Daughtry took another look at the image of the seeds before he took the flash drive out, and shut down the computer. His mind was racing with the possibilities. As soon as one popped up, he discarded it; coming to the conclusion that he didn't have an earthly clue what he was dealing with. That conclusion motivated him to hurry. He needed to get to Loren's house as quickly as possible. She

171

had to see what he was seeing. They could walk through the information together, and hopefully, come up with a reason behind this discovery.

Stuffing the computer and files into his briefcase, he punched in Loren's cell number again. It went straight to voice mail. He opened the door and glanced around the courtyard. It was empty. He locked the door behind him and walked briskly to his car. Not one given to paranoia, he couldn't shake the feeling that he was being watched. He opened the car door and slid quickly inside, cranked the car and pulled onto the street.

Feeling like a character in a get-away movie, he dialed Sailor's phone. She picked up on the first ring. "What is going on, Daughtry!"

"I'm almost home. Come to the car as soon as you see me pull up."

He disconnected before she could answer. He watched his briefcase out of the corner of his eye. The memory of the pulsing seeds loomed in his mind. He played the scenes over and over as he drove carefully down the almost deserted street to the condo. He certainly didn't want to do anything that would cause a cop to notice him. If he was stopped in the state he was in, they would probably think he was on the run from something.

When he pulled to the front of Sailor's condo, she was waiting for him. He reached across the seat and opened the door before she could grab the handle. "Get in. Let's go."

"Daughtry, you're scaring me to death! What is wrong with you?"

He gave her a brief account of what he had discovered. When questions tumbled out of her, Daughtry told her he didn't have answers. "That is why we need to talk to Loren. This is her legend. Maybe she knows more than she has shared with us. Or perhaps she knows more than she is aware of. One thing is for sure, I have never seen anything like this in my life."

Daughtry continued to drive carefully, not wanting to draw attention to their journey. Sailor prattled on, trying to drag answers out of him. Her questions went unanswered as Daughtry remained silent, staring straight ahead.

Twenty minutes later, he pulled the car into the driveway of the house where Loren was staying. She had given him the address yesterday, when they had come back from Crawfordville. He parked close to Loren's car and turned the car motor off.

He dialed her number and it went to voicemail again. They sat there a minute, staring at the dark house until Sailor said, "I see a faint light. Could be a lamp she leaves on for a nightlight."

"Well, it doesn't matter. If she is asleep, we have to wake her. This cannot keep until morning."

"You're scaring me, Daughtry. I've never seen you so shook up."

He reached over to pat her shoulder. "I don't mean to scare you, Sailor. You're right, I am, as you say, shook up." He grabbed the briefcase and said, "Let's go."

The cool night air hit them as they opened the car doors. With nerves working overtime in the spooky stillness, they softly close the doors and walked, just as quietly as possible around the garage to the back door. Praying they would not be mistaken for someone up to no good, Daughtry rapped on the door. He heard footsteps and called Loren's name. "Loren, its Daughtry. Open the door please. I need to talk to you."

Recognizing his voice, but still hesitant, Loren cracked the door leaving the night latch in place. Sailor's face peered at her. Sensing the urgency, she unlatched the chain and stepped back to let them in before she locked the door again.

She stared at their faces, and all her alarms sounded in her head, "What's happened."

Daughtry took her arm and pulled out a chair from the kitchen table. "You might want to sit down to hear what I am going to tell you."

Loren sank to the chair next to Sailor, who had sat down as soon as she came into the house. Her eyes were glued to his face.

"I've found impossibility, Loren."

"What do you mean?"

"It's the seeds. They're alive."

Loren jumped up. "Alive. They can't be. They're almost two-hundred-years-old!"

"I know the age of the seeds, Loren. I checked the data, several times. There is no mistake."

"Dear Lord, what have you discovered?"

"I have a theory. I believe Georgiana and Alice left clues. There is one thing I am certain about. I have never seen seeds that pulse with life, even though they have rested in a place that cannot produce life."

Twenty-Three

Loren stared at him, overwhelmed by his words. She wrapped her arms around her shaking body. Memories of her nightmare flashed in her mind. Deep inside, she felt the growing need to protect the quilt. "What are you saying . . . Georgiana and Alice . . . what do you mean clues?"

Before Daughtry could answer her question, she shouted, "The seeds are in danger!"

"Why do you think that," Daughtry said.

"I had a horrible nightmare last night. Someone was chasing me through dark woods. My heart was pounding against the quilt that I was holding in my arms. I was running for my life. There was a pinpoint of light up ahead in the darkness, and I knew if I could reach it I would be safe. But, I stumbled when I turned to see who was chasing me. I was falling . . . they were coming nearer . . . I couldn't move."

"Do you think my nightmare is a warning?"

A muscle jerked in his jaw. "Yes, I believe it was a warning. I have felt edgy all night. When I left the office, I couldn't shake the feeling that I was being watched."

"You two are scaring me, talking about nightmares and warnings," Sailor said.

She shivered and stood as the sound of the wind whistled through the trees near the back door. "Alright, that's enough talk about dreams and nightmare. It's giving me the heebie-jeebies."

Loren pulse raced in fear. She pushed the chair back and whispered, *be quiet!* She stood close to Sailor and said, "Listen, I heard something out front!"

Daughtry frowned. "I didn't hear anything."

They followed him as he walked towards the front door. He reached to open it. His hand stopped in midair as he heard footsteps. He hissed, "Get down." Loren and Sailor dropped to their knees.

"Shush," he whispered in the darkness. He motioned for them to crawl into the narrow hallway connecting the kitchen to the den. They obeyed. Daughtry closed the door and leaned against the wall before he spoke. "Someone's out there."

"Oh, God. Now I'm really scared," Sailor whispered.

"We can't take any chances. Loren, you said in your nightmare that someone was chasing you to get the quilt. Maybe that someone is outside your door right now."

With her heart hammering in her chest, Loren whispered, "The quilt is on my bed. I have to get it!"

"Don't stand up. Whoever is outside may see you through the window."

He signaled for them to stay put. "I'll check the front of the house to see if they're still there." He crouched down and slowly duck-walked through the dining room into the living room. He peeked out the window. He could barely make out the shadow of a SUV. It was parked across the road, partially hidden by the large oak trees on the empty lot, two doors down from Loren's house. Two men were standing at the back of the car smoking. He could see the glow of their cigarettes. He let the curtain fall back into place and crawled back.

He told them what he had seen. "Loren, go get the quilt and the journal. Stay down and hurry. We need to get out of here before daylight"

Loren could feel the cold sweat running down the middle of her back as she crawled towards the bedroom. Everything around her turned into a blur. The bile rose into her throat. She stopped when she heard a car door slam. She swallowed. *Oh, God, help me!*

She found the bed in the limited light, and grabbed the quilt and the journal. She checked to make sure Grammas' letter was in the journal. It was. She wadded the quilt as tightly as she could. Her breath came out in shaky gasps as she crawled back.

Daughtry and Sailor met her in the kitchen. She gave him the journal. He put it in his briefcase. "We need to get out of here. Daylight is coming, and we will be sitting ducks," said Daughtry.

All their instincts kicked in. The room had gone silent – like everything was holding its breath. They stopped, listening. Not even the air was stirring. After a moment they moved, keeping close to the floor, listening to the sounds around them.

They crouched lower to the floor and waited. A few moments later, they moved forward. They reached the back door. Daughtry rose up on one knee to turn the doorknob. He slowly opened it enough to look out. He turned to Loren and Sailor and eyed them carefully. This was make or break time.

"I don't hear anyone out back. It's still dark enough we can make a run for it. When I open the door, head for the trees along the property line and don't stop until I tell you to."

"Let me go first. If I see anyone, I'll run the other way to throw them off," Sailor offered.

Daughtry looked her in the eye. "Are you sure about that?"

"Yes, Loren has the quilt. You have the flash drive and the journal. They need to be protected. Let me do this. I want to."

Daughtry opened the door wider, and Sailor slipped out into the night. She raced across the slippery grass that was wet from the nighttime dew. Moments later, Daughtry told Loren to run. "Go into the trees, I'll be right behind you."

She ran, clutching the quilt. She prayed the footsteps she could hear behind her belonged to Daughtry. She found the cover of the hanging limbs, and continued to run with the quilt held tightly against her racing heart. She stumbled, falling headlong on top of Sailor who was waiting ahead of her. They scrambled up, trying to catch their breath.

"Thank God, it's you, Sailor. Did you see anyone?"

Daughtry touched them on the arm. "Quiet!" He looked back toward the house they'd just left. He didn't see anyone.

"Okay. Whoever is out front must not have seen us leave. That doesn't mean we are safe. There are a couple of problems. Our cars are in plain sight, so we can't go to them. We are too far out of town to walk, and that wouldn't be wise anyway. I suppose the best we can do is stay in the trees until we come up with a better plan."

Loren turned her head, trying to get her bearings. She pointed to a house several doors down where the tree line ended. "That's Mr. Frank's house. A light is on in his kitchen."

"Do you know him?" whispered Daughtry.

"Yes, he's a good friend of Doug and Leta's. He called to say he had promised them he'd keep an eye on me while they're gone," said Loren.

"Sssh . . . listen, said Daughtry, raising his hand, and motioning for them to freeze. He whispered to them and pointed, "I hear something over there."

They held their breath, not daring to move. They saw a small black and white pug-bulldog. His nose was to the ground, and he was slowly wobbling their way. He got within inches of their hiding place before he threw back his head and let out a feeble bark.

"Go away!" Daughtry hissed. The dog continued to bark with short squeaky sounds that reminded him of someone's fingernails scraping on a blackboard. He was close enough for them to see that he was old. His rheumy, black eyes were clouded, and the loose folds of skin hung around his round body as he stood his ground.

"Oh brother, he thinks he's a big, bad dog!"

181

"That's Mr. Frank's dog," Loren whispered.

The dog didn't budge until they heard someone calling, "Sam, here boy!" The dog gave an answering bark and stood still, staring at the three people huddled in the trees.

"There you are, boy. You know you're not supposed to run off like that."

Loren recognized her neighbor as he bent over to attach the leash to the dog collar. She slipped out of the trees to face him as he straightened up. "Loren, what are you doing hiding in the trees?"

"Hey, Mr. Frank, I need your help."

"What's wrong? Do I need to call 911 for you?"

"No sir, I need a place to hide. My friends do too."

Releasing their breath, Daughtry and Sailor stepped out so Mr. Carter could see them. He looked from one to the other. "Well now, what have we here?"

Throwing caution to the wind, Daughtry decided to take a chance on his good reputation. With daylight coming they needed to find cover soon. Reaching out his hand, he said, "I'm Dr. Daughtry Corbin."

Mr. Carter narrowed his eyes and said, "Dr. Corbin, I recognize you sir. I attended a couple of your lectures here in Tallahassee."

Picking up the pug, Frank motioned to them, "Bring your friends to the house, Loren. If a hiding place is needed, I can provide that for the time being."

"Thank you, Mr. Frank. Let's get in the house and I'll explain what is happening."

As they walked close behind him to the house, a spark of interest rose in the retired detective. Frank Carter was nobody's fool. He'd seen and heard too many lame stories over the forty-plus years he'd worked the streets of New York. He recognized the truth when it was staring him in the face.

Besides, he'd felt a connection to Loren since the first time he'd met her. He imagined it was the same connection a father would feel for his daughter. Since he had never married, and didn't have a daughter, he couldn't be sure. All he knew for certain, was that he enjoyed her company and wanted to make sure everything was alright.

Twenty-Four

The smell of coffee welcomed them as they went into the kitchen. Frank put Sam down in a pet bed near a counter that separated the kitchen from the pantry. The little dog made several circles, nudging the padding with his nose, and then dropped down with his head on his paws. He promptly closed his eyes, exhaling soft snores as he drifted to sleep.

Frank looked at him with affection. "Poor old fellow, he's tuckered out. He doesn't have a lot of spunk these days."

Frank felt the tension electrifying the room. All of his instincts kicked into gear. Trouble was brewing. His three guest stood huddled, Loren in the middle, with a bed quilt grasped in her arms. To Frank, she looked like she was holding onto it like a drowning person would hold a life preserver.

"Loren, you wanna tell me what's going on here?"

She gulped in air. "There's a black SUV parked down the street with two men. They're watching the house, and we believe they are going to break into it. We got scared and ran."

"Why?"

She looked at Daughtry, then at Sailor. "Just because . . . we're scared."

185

"I'll call 911 for you. If there's going to be a break-in, you need the cops on the way," Frank declared.

He didn't miss the frantic look they exchanged.

"No, don't call the police. We don't want the cops involved" Daughtry said.

"Okay, but the irony is, I am a cop. Do I need to leave the room?" Frank said with a chuckle.

Frank thought they looked like they were about to bolt. He held up his arms in surrender. "Okay...no cops. Loren, do you have a Security Alarm System?"

"We do, but I turned it off when Daughtry and Sailor arrived. I didn't think about re-arming it before we ran."

"Okay. Probably wouldn't keep a determined person out anyway. The bad guys always find a way to do their dirty work," Frank declared with a grimace.

"Now, tell me your story. I need to know what I'm dealing with."

Loren said, "It will probably sound like a wild story to you."

"No problem. I've heard wild stories before," Frank declared.

"We need to protect this quilt. We think the people watching the house want to steal it."

For the life of him, Frank couldn't see a quilt as a reason for a break-in. He knew antique quilts were valued by collectors but this one, while very pretty, just looked like a common quilt to him.

Daughtry joined the conversation. "The quilt Loren is holding is not an ordinary quilt. It protects a Legend of Promise that her family has guarded for two centuries. We have a suspicion that some of them have sacrificed their lives to keep it safe. That suspicion has grown surer after what happened just now at Loren's house. We believe there is someone, or perhaps more than one person, who would like to steal the quilt. We think those people were outside her house and would have come after the quilt, even if it meant killing us to get it. That's why we ran. We had to get away before they found us. We were hiding in the trees, trying to decide what to do next when your dog spotted us."

Frank was enough of a professional to keep a straight face, even in the wake of a cock-and-bull story like this. "That's it? You're telling me that you all are on the run from the bad guys, who you believe are willing to kill you for a bed quilt?"

"Yes, that's what I'm telling you. It's the truth."

Something in the tone of Daughtrys' voice spoke to a place deep inside of the aged detective, who had long given up on the miraculous. His days and nights on the streets of a city where crime ran rampant, had hardened what little belief he had ever had in anything, other than what he could explain with facts. Sure, he'd been witness, a time or two, to things that didn't fit, but he figured they were a coincidence, or just plain good luck.

But on the other hand, he had a lot of respect for the doctor. He'd followed his work, and knew him to be a man of science, so he owned it to him to listen with an open mind.

"Okay, Dr. Corbin, you've got my ear. What's the rest of the story?"

"I'll let Loren pick it up from here. This is really her story to tell," said Daughtry.

Frank saw Sam amble over to Loren who had sat down. She picked the dog up and put him in her lap, on top of the quilt. He was shocked to see his dog snuggle against the quilt. He was even more shocked to watch the dog lying there contented, as Loren petted him.

"Well, looks like old Sam has made a friend."

Loren smiled, and continued to pet the dog as she told her story. Watching Frank's face to see his reaction, she outlined the events that had brought them to today's circumstance. Her eyes watered with tears at the retelling of Grammas' sudden death. She told him about the discovery of the family Promise that had been hidden from her, and what they had learned in the few days she had known Daughtry and Sailor.

She concluded her story with last night's nightmare, and the discovery of the seeds that were very much alive. "The findings on the seeds are why Daughtry and Sailor were at my house. He had just finished showing me the seeds on the flash drive. They pulse with life. We heard a sound outside. We realized we could be in danger. That's when we grabbed the quilt and ran."

Frank measured every word she spoke by the years of his experience. The story didn't add up to him. But, experience had taught him to be a patient man when following a lead. He figured he knew Loren well enough to trust her word, even if it did sound like a far-out tale.

On the other hand, if the story was true and they were in danger, he couldn't ignore their plea for help.

Before he could speak, Sam jumped down from Loren's lap. He yipped and bounced around the kitchen, ending up beside Frank, where he continued to bounce up and down like a pup.

"Well I never . . . look at you . . . what in the world has gotten into you, Sam?"

The excited dog jumped onto Frank's lap, and began covering his chin with doggy kisses. Overcome with emotion, he rubbed the dog's back, trying to calm him down.

Loren stroked the quilt, feeling the tingles running up her arms, as she watched the little dog behaving as if he'd been reborn.

"He touched the quilt. That's why he's acting like he is."

Daughtry and Sailor moved closer to Loren. "Just like Grayson except without the sparkles," Sailor chimed in.

Frank caught their words over the playful dog's barks. He looked at them with eyebrows raised. "What do you mean about sparkles? Is there more to the story than what you've told me?"

"There's more. We just didn't know that the quilt would affect animals the same way it does humans," Loren said gently.

"You're telling me the quilt in your lap, has something to do with old Sam's behavior."

"That's what I believe. Yesterday, we watched a three-year-old change from a sickly child, to one glowing with renewed health. It happened after he touched the quilt. Just like Sam, he changed instantly."

Daring to put an ounce of trust in the unknown, Frank gingerly reached over and caught hold of the quilt with both hands. The buzz he felt was apparent on his face, before he uttered a soft, "Wow, what was that!"

Twenty-Five

Less than thirty minutes had passed since they had made their get-away. During that time, they had been rescued and seen the healing of a small animal. They'd also seen a crusty old retired detective willing to take a chance on something he'd never seen before.

His offer to take them in had been extended to an offer to help them in whatever way was needed. Loren knew God was at work. Grammas' soft words hummed in her heart. She had constantly reminded Loren that God was a Father to the fatherless, and that he would never leave nor forsake her.

Frank stared at them with the intensity of someone looking at a line-up of *America's Most Wanted*. "Here's the plan; I'm gonna mosey out the front to see if the bad guys are still lurking down the road. If they are, I'll call the hotline for Tallahassee Police Department that there's a suspicious vehicle in the neighborhood. You folks need to sit tight, right here in my kitchen until I check the street out. Then we'll lay out the rest of the plan."

They watched as Frank pulled out a revolver from a shoulder holster, flipped the loaded chamber open and checked it. He slipped it back in the holster and said, "Stay put. This won't take long."

The look of stunned surprise on Daughtry, Loren and Sailor's faces brought a smile to his lips. They were obviously amateurs in the field of *good guys versus bad guys*. If he took on their cause, he'd need to toughen them up a bit or they would be a liability to his safety.

Almost immediately he saw the coast was clear. It was too early for the neighborhood to be stirring, and if a black SUV was still around it had changed its parking place. He followed Sam, who was acting like he could run a mile. Frank chuckled and said. "Settle down, little man. We're on a surveillance mission."

To the average observer, they were just a man and his dog, out for an early morning stroll. But, looks were deceiving, Frank didn't miss a thing. His trained mind calculated every movement and every sound.

He couldn't put a finger on it, but he felt different. He felt renewed, energetic. The tingle he'd experienced when he touched Loren's quilt, still vibrated in his body. He looked at Sam trotting in front of him like he was leading a parade. He smiled, wondering if he had the same look of pleased pleasure on his face. He lifted his hands to see that they still looked the same. The lines of age were still visible...but deep inside he knew a change had taken place. He felt at peace with himself and the world around him, for the first time in his life.

Satisfied that the SUV that Daughtry had spotted last night was gone, he called Sam and returned to his house.

Back in the kitchen, Frank found the group still frozen in place. Fear lined their faces. They stood rigid, waiting for Frank to speak. "The SUV is gone. Course, that doesn't guarantee the bad guys are gone. We best be getting out of here soon as we can."

Loren swallowed her fear and gulped, "We...what are you talking about?"

"Look, I've got a feeling that whoever is after you will be back. You can't hide out in my kitchen forever. Both of your cars are in front of your house. If someone's watching, and I believe they are, you can't get to your car without being seen. My car is in the garage. I'm offering you a ride out of here."

"Why would you do that?"

"Loren, I certainly don't understand all the ins and outs of your quilt, but one thing I do understand is the effect it had on Sam . . . and me. I haven't been this excited to be alive in twenty-five years. If someone wants it for the wrong reason, I plan to stand in their way."

Loren felt the sweet peace of God flood her soul. God had provided a way of escape. Hope replaced her fear. Joy burst in her heart. "Your offer is accepted. Tell us what we need to do."

"I don't know how sophisticated your pursuers are, but we need to make sure we don't leave a trail they can follow. Do you have a cell phone," Frank asked?

"I do," Daughtry said.

"You need to trash it. Cell phones can be traced."

"Can I check my messages first?"

193

"No, if you need to make a call, we'll stop at a Stop and Shop Store and pick up a pre-pay phone. What about you two?"

Loren and Sailor shook their heads. "I think I left my phone on the table by Jack's cage....Oh no....Jack has to be fed, I can't just leave him," Loren wailed in distress.

"That's Doug and Leta's bird, isn't it?"

"Yes, and they love him. What can I do?"

"Birds don't eat that much. He'll be fine today. Is there someone you can call once we are on the road?"

Loren thought a minute. She could call Carolyn, but she would ask a million questions. People's faces raced through her mind. "I know. I'll call Noah. He's the teenager who mows the yard. I'll tell him I had to go home for a few days and could he please look after Jack. He knows where the spare key is kept. He's taken care of Jack when Doug and Leta were on vacation."

"Good idea. Now, does anybody have any cash," Frank asked?

Daughtry pulled out his wallet, "I've got a couple of hundred."

"What about you girls?"

"I grabbed my purse when we ran this morning, but I don't have a lot of cash in it," Loren said.

"Same for me," Sailor said, as she checked her small shoulder bag that hung across her chest.

"No problem if you have your ATM cards. We can make a stop on the way out of town."

Frank asked where they banked, and discovered they used different banks. He figured that was a good thing since he could drive from one side of town, to the other side. If anyone was watching the neighborhood, and saw him leaving, they might decide to put a tail on his car. They could do that, but Frank had years of experience in losing a tail. He hadn't forgotten the tricks of his trade.

"Okay, I'm gonna pack a small bag. Why don't you all get that basket out of the utility room and throw some snacks in it. The less we need to stop, the better off we'll be," Frank said, as he turned to leave the kitchen.

"Mr. Frank, are you sure you want to do this? I don't know what might happen or even where we need to go."

He took her hand and looked her squarely in the eyes. "Loren, I've lived a good life. Made all the money I need. I figure it's time I pay back some of the debt to whoever allowed me to do and have the things I've had. Something happened this morning. I can't put a name to it, but I feel different, like hope has been renewed. I've never settled in my mind the possibility of this 'God' that most folks take for granted. Maybe it's time I decide what I believe. Could be, this little journey might be the time I find the answers to a whole lot of questions I've never been brave enough to ask before."

He's a lost soul searching for the truth. He needs you as much as you need him!

Loren smiled and said, "Okay, Mr. Frank. We're ready when you are."

Twenty-Six

They held each other's gaze for a moment. Frank nodded, "Alright, here's what we're looking at. If the folks who are interested in your quilt wanted to steal it, they probably would have already done so. That makes me think the guys you saw are a couple of goons who were sent to check out your house. They must have cleared out before morning. On the other hand, you don't need to take a chance by going back to your house or driving your car. Dr. Corbin, your car is out as well; since I'm sure they spotted it last night."

"I have some cash and a full tank of gas. Credit cards are too dangerous to use, but we should get a pass on a debit card. The thing is, we don't know how sophisticated the folks are that are after you. If they're on the level of the two last night, we'll be okay. But, my gut tells me the higher up the chain of command the smarter they'll be," Frank said.

"Frank, we appreciate this. As you know, Loren doesn't have any family left to help her, and all of mine and Sailor's family are hundreds of miles away. This is not the kind of thing you make plans for," Daughtry replied.

"Enough said. Fact is, you need a ride out of here and I could use a vacation. We'll make our get-away together. On down the road, you can buy a cheap cell with a prepaid card. Those stay under the radar pretty well, making them harder to trace."

197

Daughtry found several cases of bottled water in the pantry. He stacked some bottles on the counter and stood to the side to watch the girls fill the basket with boxes of crackers and fruit. "Frank's a veteran at this, so I guess we should trust his judgment. He said the less we have to stop, the safer it'll be for us. We also need to avoid public places since we have no idea where these guys might show up. All this cloak and dagger stuff makes me feel like I'm in a spy movie."

"I wonder if they are from Tallahassee. If they are, they could have been watching us for a while." Sailor shuddered and said, "I feel like I'm being stalked!"

Frank swung his bag to his shoulder and headed back to the kitchen. Daughtry stood with his feet planted apart. He held his briefcase tightly against his side. A scowl furrowed his brow. This was way beyond what he wanted to be doing.

"Frank, I don't know if this is the best thing to do, man. I'm having second thoughts about the wisdom of running off like this."

"Look, Dr. Corbin, I respect your opinion, and I respect your concern. But, this is my area of expertise. I believe you all need to distance yourselves from here, until you learn more about the source of the danger. My gut tells me the danger is still there. You need to trust me. Let me do my job. I've been in these circumstances before and I know what can happen. We need to go."

Loren moved behind Daughtry. She placed her hand on his arm. "He's right; we can't sit here waiting for those guys to return. The next time they might do more than just watch us. They could kill us!"

With a look of panic on her face Sailor grabbed the basket of food. "Sounds like a plan I can live with. Let's go."

Frank opened the car door. "Okay, ladies settle in. I'll show you how to make a clean get-away," he joked. He slid under the wheel, and Sam crawled onto his lap.

Before he raised the garage door, he told his passengers to slide down out of sight until they were outside of Tallahassee. He pressed the remote to open the door, backed the car to the end of the driveway. He stopped and checked the spot where they had seen the SUV parked last night.

"Looks like your guys were working the graveyard shift. They must have called the watch off. There's nobody there this morning."

He glanced over at Daughtry, whose lanky body was folded like a crumpled napkin in the passenger seat. He chuckled.

"Sorry about the uncomfortable ride. I'll make sure we don't pick up a tail, and then you all can come up for air." Daughtry echoed Loren and Sailor's spoken okay with a thumb up sign.

The ride out of Tallahassee took on a surreal quality for Loren, as Frank maneuvered the Escalade through traffic, with the ease of an experienced driver. He pulled into the drive-thru at First National and told Loren the coast was clear. She inserted her card, and requested an amount

199

of cash. By the time Frank drove away from the bank, Loren's nerves were screaming. She sank back against the seat, shaking from head to toe.

"Hold steady, Loren. There's not a bad guy in sight," Frank reassured her as he watched her in the rearview mirror of the car.

He drove across town to Commercial Bank where Daughtry and Sailor made withdrawals. As he headed back to town, he said, "The ideal situation would be to have a car that doesn't belong in our neighborhood. We don't know how smart these folks are. If they are any good at the game, they would check out the car registrations, figuring you all had to hitch a ride out of town. So, a change of plan is in order."

"What kind of change?"

Frank rubbed his chin as he said, "I have the keys to my buddy Bucks' car. He's out in the wilds of Alaska on a month long fishing trip. We'll make a swap. I'll leave the Escalade at his house and use his car for our trip."

Satisfied with his plan, Frank turned off the four-lane and headed out of Tallahassee. About fifteen minutes later, he made a turn onto a dirt driveway that led into a heavily, wooded area. The house sat about a half mile from the road. It was completely concealed by a privacy fence. Frank stopped, punched in a code on the gate, and it swung open. He hit a remote on his key-ring that opened the double garage, and pulled the Escalade inside.

"Come on ladies, we've got a new ride."

Loren and Sailor scooted across the seat, grabbing their purses as they went. Loren tucked the quilt under her arm. Her heart was drumming. She scrambled in the back seat and slammed the door.

"Oh, God help me not to panic . . . I'm alright . . . breathe, Loren, breathe," she muttered to herself.

Sailor slid across the seat and noticed her fear. She gently patted her arm. "Look, Loren, there's no one here. We're okay."

"I know. I just feel like someone is watching our every move."

"Well, they're not. We are in the middle of the woods. There's no one here but the coons and the squirrels. They can't harm you."

Sailor pulled the quilt from under Loren's arm and tucked it around her. Frank and Daughtry put the basket with the food and Frank's overnight bag in the back of the car. Taking deep breaths to calm herself, she felt the familiar tingles as she laid her head back against the seat. Frank slid under the wheel of the Crossover with Sam perched on his lap and said, "Buckle up folks. We're on our way."

He drove back down the lane and pulled onto the road that led them to Interstate Ten. By the time they merged with the mid-day traffic, they all took a relieved breath when Frank told them it didn't look like they had been followed.

Settling back against the seat, she listened as the others rehashed the events that had brought them to this point. Loren's thoughts were on the quilt. There was no turning back now. She knew she would protect the quilt and the legend it carried, with her life if necessary. She ran her hands across the fabric. The contact brought comfort. She mused about the possibility of Georgiana caressing it in the same way during a crisis. Her thoughts raced ahead to the other Grandmothers, who very likely had encountered trying times as well. Lastly, her mind settled on her Mama. Her hand stilled on the quilt. She imagined a hand holding hers, pouring strength and resolve into her soul. A smile tugged at the corners of her lips.

She would be okay; God would provide whatever they needed. Thinking about her Mama and God working together on her behalf comforted her...calmed her.

. . .

The blast of a car horn startled Loren. She ducked low in the seat when Frank shouted, *get down!*

Loren stared at Sailor in silence as the car swerved sharply to the right. "Hang on," Frank said as he corrected the path of the car. They heard a loud whoosh as a car passed close to them, accelerated and changed lanes.

"Well, lookee here. A black SUV headed somewhere in a hurry. If it's the one you saw last night, it could be your bad guys heading out of town too. **NHL 612.** Looks like a Louisiana license plate buried under a pile of dirt."

Daughtry slowly lifted his head. He had ducked down in the seat when Frank warned them to hide. He watched the SUV whip in and out of the traffic. "I can't be one-hundred percent sure, but it looks like the one I saw last night."

"Well, if the Florida Highway Patrol doesn't stop them for speeding, or if they don't end up in a ditch, they should arrive where they're going pretty soon."

"Now then, perhaps it's time for you to let me know where we're headed, as well," Frank declared.

Daughtry twisted around in the seat to face Loren and Sailor. "I have a destination in mind, but we haven't discussed it yet."

"Well, speak it out son. Interstate Ten runs all the way from Florida to California. We need to know what you have in mind."

"Okay, here's my plan. Loren, you know I told you that our ancestor, Alice, moved to New Orleans with Pastor Smith and his family. Well, Sailor and I have scads of relatives scattered all the way from Baton Rouge to the bayous of the Gulf of Mexico. We can get lost from the outside world for as long as we need to in Louisiana. No questions asked."

"That's a perfect plan! No one knows the bayou country like our family does," Sailor said.

Loren had been whispering prayers for guidance, as she listened to them talking. She remembered how Georgiana had loved her friend, Alice, from the time they had shared a cradle together. Alice had helped Georgiana hide the seeds in the wedding quilt, and had been a comfort to her when Richard died in the War. Two centuries later,

Loren believed God had led her to Alice's grandchildren when the quilt was facing danger again. They had come full-circle; Georgiana and Alice's ancestors were together again through their grandchildren. She knew, with certainty, it was where they were being led to go.

"Louisiana sounds like the perfect place to go."

"Well, ladies and gentleman, it's your decision; I'm just along for the ride. There's just one catch with your plan. If the boys riding in that SUV up ahead are the ones who were watching your house, and if they are headed to Louisiana as well, then chances are we could all end up in the same place," Frank cautioned.

Loren never blinked an eye as she remembered one of her favorite Bible verses.

"Even though I walk through the valley of the shadow of death, I will fear no evil, for my God is with me.

"God will protect us. It's where He wants us to go, Loren said."

Twenty-Seven

"It's your call, Loren. I see the confidence in you. And, you are absolutely right. God walks before us," Daughtry said.

"Yay! We're going home! You'll love our family, Loren. And you will too, Mr. Frank. We'll feast on crawdads and all kinds of yummy concoctions, "Sailor said, as she bubbled over with excitement.

"Oh, it's a mighty fine place to eat, all right. If we'd made this trip a little sooner, we could have been there for Mardi Gras. I've enjoyed that celebration a few times. I've got a friend with the Bureau who lives there. We stay in touch. Could be I'll call old Colt to see what he's up to," Frank said.

"What division of the Bureau is he with," Daughtry asked.

"He's a U.S. Marshal. He started out as a rookie at N.Y.P.D. Good man. He knows how to work a case from all angles. His work on a terrorist's plot, while he was with the police department in New York, got the attention of Washington D.C. They offered him a job, right after that."

Frank tapped his fingers against the steering wheel, lost in thought. "Yes sir just might need to see if Marshal Colton Shaw has any information on the guys riding in the SUV ahead of us. He has access to a data base some of us can only dream about, and he'd be a good man to have on board with us."

The others cast nervous glances towards each other as Frank told them about his friend. It was evident in their eyes that the adventure they were a part of was quickly becoming more than they had imagined. Daughtry pulled his briefcase closer to him, clicked it open and started to boot up the computer.

Frank stuck out his hand and said, "Nope, don't do that Dr. Corbin. Not a smart thing to do. Internet can be traced. There is a way to save your data and erase the history. But, it'd be wise to hold off until we can take care of that."

Daughtry sighed. "I wasn't thinking. I knew better than to do that. Nerves . . . habit . . . whatever, it won't happen again."

"Let's pull off and get some lunch. It's nearly one o'clock. With all this switch-a-roo we're running late. Sound good to you all?"

"I'm in agreement. How about you two," Sailor asked. Daughtry and Loren nodded yes.

Frank slowed down to exit and pulled into a drive-thru. He said the Louisiana state line was another five or six hours down the road. They could make it by night if they kept driving.

"Yay, we'll be at our parent's house by supper time. Only problem is, they don't know we're coming," Sailor complained.

Looking around to check the area out, Frank slowly pulled into a fast food restaurant. They gave their order for burger and fries, paid and crossed over to a Quick-Stop.

"I'll top the gas tank off. You guys run in and get a pre-paid phone. You might want to make a pit-stop before we hit the road again. The less we stop, the faster we can get to your folks house."

Back on the road, Daughtry added the minutes to his phone and handed it to Sailor so she could call their parents. Her face lit up with a smile when she heard her Mama's soft hello.

"Hey, Mama, how are you? Yes mam, we're fine. Listen, Mama, Daughtry and I are coming to see you. Yes, mam, today. We have a couple of friends with us. I told them you wouldn't mind company. Okay, Mama, see you at supper time. Love you. Bye."

"She's happy. She says we don't visit enough."

"What caused you and Daughtry to fly away from home," Frank asked?

"Looking for our identity, I suppose. It's hard to be an individual when you are part of a large family like ours," Sailor said.

"Do they live in New Orleans?"

"No, they live in Mandeville on the North Shore of Lake Pontchartrain. Our Dad is a doctor. He worked at Southeast Louisiana Hospital before he retired. Most of our family lives in Metairie in Jefferson Parrish. Our Cajun ancestors settled in the area way back in the 1700's. The rest of them are in smaller fishing villages along the coast."

207

Frank glanced at his passengers, who looked like they were on the verge of collapsing. "Why don't you three get some shut-eye. Chances are it could be another long night."

"Good idea. I just need to make one call," Daughtry said as he keyed in Nikki's number.

Her voice mail picked up. "Nikki, this is Daughtry. Call this number as soon as possible. Something's come up and I really need to talk to you."

He'd barely hug up when the phone rang. He answered. "Yes, listen Nikki . . . what, Oh my Lord . . . the doctors are sure . . . I am overjoyed for you. Now, Nikki, listen to me. I discovered something about the seeds in Loren's quilt that could be responsible for Grayson's healing. Sailor and I were at Loren's house last night, and we believe someone was watching the house. We think they were after the quilt, so we ran. We are going away until this dies down. You need to leave too, Nikki. I'm sorry; I believe you and Grayson will be in danger if the people find out about Grayson being healed from leukemia. Okay, that's a good place, go there and don't tell anyone what is going on except his Dad. I love you too. Bye and I'll call later."

Loren and Sailor listened to Daughtrys' side of the conversation. They were grinning. "Is it true . . . the leukemia is gone," Loren whispered.

"Yes, Nikki said the doctors are stumped. The best they could come up with was that sometimes it goes into remission, but usually returns."

"It won't return. God healed Grayson," Sailor declared joyfully!

"Will someone let me in on this conversation," Frank suggested.

Daughtry told him that Nikki and Grayson were his and Sailor's cousins. Then he told him about the way Grayson was affected by the quilt at his lab after they had completed the carbon-dating.

"We saw Grayson change from a sickly-pale child, to a rosy-cheeked three-year-old, brimming with good health. Nikki took him to the doctor today and they said they could not find a trace of the disease."

"What did she tell the doctors?"

"Nothing. She didn't say anything. Just acted stunned. She had told Grayson not to tell them about the quilt, that it was their secret."

"She's leaving Tallahassee?"

"Yes, right now. Her ex-husband lives in Miami. They stay in touch because of Grayson. She'll go there. They'll keep her safe."

"The plot thickens, and we don't know what could be waiting at the end of the road. Go to sleep, I'll wake you when we are almost there," concluded Frank.

He waited until he was sure they were sleeping before he punched in the private number for his friend and former partner, Colton Shaw. Colt picked up on the first ring.

"What's happening, man," he said.

"Well, hello to you as well," Frank chuckled.

"You calling for pleasure or a problem," Colt returned.

"It's always a pleasure, and I hope we don't have too much of a problem. Need a favor. I'm tailing a black SUV. Plate number **NLH 612.** Check it out for me, son, and give me a call back."

"You got it. Hey, by the way, where are you?"

"Would you believe I'm about a couple of hours from the Louisiana state line," Frank said.

"No kidding. You coming to see me? I'll get the boat gassed up and break out the fishing rods."

"Aw, man, how I'd like to pull one of those old redfish out of the Gulf. But, it'll have to wait until I take care of a wee bit of a problem. I have three passengers who could be in a world of trouble. Don't have all the details worked out yet but I've got a feeling this could turn into something ugly."

"I hear you, bud. Bingo . . . got a hit on the tag. It's registered to a company by the name of Premier Pharmaceutical's right here in the Big Easy."

"Well, how about that. It looks like there could be a whole lot more to this than I thought."

"Okay, I recognize that tone. What's up?"

"Better not discuss it over the phone. We're headed to Mandeville. I'll call you from there. Bye, Son."

Frank felt the stare coming from Daughtry before he turned to look him in the eye. "You heard?"

"Yes, I heard most of the conversation. It sounds like you're concerned for our safety."

"I ain't gonna sugar-coat it Doc. Red flags are going up all over the place for me. Somebody is going to a lot of trouble over a quilt. I'm gonna pull over to the next Rest Area. You can drive the rest of the way, since you know where we're going."

He exited the Interstate about five minutes later and pulled into the Rest Area. He got out, looked around and decided it was clear. He curled his thumb and forefinger in the Okay sign to Daughtry through the car window. Daughtry and the girls, who were just waking up, climbed out of the car, stretched, and made their way to the bathrooms.

Frank trailed behind them, and paused to answer the phone. Colt's number showed on the ID.

"Yep. Whatcha got?"

"Pretty interesting stuff, that's what I've got. The SUV is registered to the owner of Premier Pharmaceutical. His name is Jude Smith. The word out is that he thinks he's above the arm of the law. He uses his flunky's to do his dirty work, keeping his hands clean. The department is itching to see him make a mistake, but so far he's not obliged them. Whatever he's up to, you can take it to the bank, it's no good. You need to watch your back. This guy is bad news!"

Frank heard the click ending Colton's call. He watched Daughtry, Loren and Sailor walking to the car, and wondered how much of this latest information he needed to share with them. One thing he knew for sure was that their lives were in danger, and the purveyor of that danger now had a name . . . Jude Smith!

Twenty-Eight

Frank tossed Daughtry the keys. "Let's get in and you can pull over to the end of the parking lot. We need to talk, before we go any further."

Sailor and Loren locked eyes with Daughtry. The tension between them was thick enough to cut with a knife. They slid into the car without saying a word, and Daughtry eased the car towards the deserted section of the Rest Area.

When he'd shut the motor off, Frank turned in the seat to face Daughtry. "My buddy called from New Orleans. He got a hit on the SUV. It belongs to a rich guy who owns a good portion of the real estate in the city. Guys name is Jude Smith."

Daughtry looked at Sailor. She sputtered, "What! Jude Smith! Are you saying he's the one behind this scare tactic?"

"Why? Do you all know this guy?"

Daughtry held his hand up to silence Sailor, whose face was scrunched up in a fierce scowl. He knew her well enough to see that she was about to burst with anger. He looked at Frank and said, "Yes, we know a person named Jude Smith. Maybe it's not the same one."

"Well, let's see if it matches my guy. According to Colt, this Mr. Smith is a self-made millionaire, who is the

213

head of a very successful company named Premier Pharmaceuticals."

Sailor beat on the back of the seat with her fist and let out a slow moan. "Daughtry . . . ?"

"Hold on a minute, Sailor. Okay, yes, it appears this is the same man we know. In fact, our family friendship goes back two centuries. Our ancestor, Alice, moved to Louisiana with his ancestor William Smith."

"Well now, it wouldn't be the first time I've seen the enemy be a bosom buddy. Let's just chill out, and when we get to your folks house, I'll get with Colt and see what he has on our Jude Smith."

"Jude, my foot! It's more like Judas, if you ask me. He's betrayed our family!" Sailor exclaimed still seething with anger.

Loren sat quietly, listening to their conversation. Her thoughts were scattered. She felt vulnerable. She had trusted Daughtry and Sailor, and now it seemed her trust could have been a mistake. If they knew the person who was putting her life in danger, it could be because they had let them know where she was. Her heartbeat sounded loudly in her ears. Maybe they were taking her straight to him. She moaned.

Sailor heard her and said, "Loren, what is it?"

Loren shrank back into the corner of the car seat. A look of panic covered her face.

Seeing the look on her face, Sailor reached her hand to her and said, "Oh, Loren, I promise you, we don't have anything to do with this. Please believe me!"

"Let's all take a breath. We don't need to borrow trouble. I've got your back on this, Loren," Frank reassured her.

Daughtry adjusted the seat and said, "Are we ready to travel? I have a few questions for Jude myself."

"Let's go, but I don't think it would be wise to contact the guy until we get a few more details on this. Could be someone stole the SUV, and Mr. Smith is totally unaware of where they were" Frank said.

They rode in silence for several miles. Frank turned the new information over in his mind. He wanted to believe that the Doc and his sister were on the up and up, but on the other hand, he'd seen evil that looked good on more than one occasion. He sure hoped he was wrong, but he needed to keep an open mind, just in case he had the jack-rabbits who were out to hurt Loren, riding in the car with him.

Putting that line of thinking aside, he looked at Loren. Her face was pale. He'd seen shock plenty of times, and she looked like she could be tottering on the edge of it. He needed to get her mind headed in another direction, so he asked, "Have you ever visited the Crescent City?"

"Yes," she said softly.

"That's good. It's a beautiful city that never sleeps. Why I remember one time when a bunch of us stayed up for days celebrating Mardi Gras. We were on the way to jail until the cops figured out he was dealing with a bunch of fellow cops," Frank chuckled.

A smile curved the corners of her mouth. "I love Mardi Gras too. And, I love the architecture of the French

Quarter. It is very unique. Gramma and I stayed at a different Bed and Breakfast each time we came. One day, we had driven to Baton Rouge to visit the restored plantations on the river. The time got away from us and it was close to midnight when we boarded the Belle Chasse ferry to cross the Mississippi River. It was a magic time," Loren said.

They sat up straighter as Daughtry crossed Lake Pontchartrain. He made the circle, leaving the city to their left, and about twenty minutes later he turned the car into the driveway of a cream, two-story house with dark green shutters. Flowers bloomed in abundance along both sides of the spacious front porch.

"We're home!" Sailor declared with joy.

Frank opened the car door right about the time Maurice and Emilie Corbin peeked out their front door. Seeing the look of concern on his Mama's face when she didn't recognize the car, Daughtry opened the car door and called out, "It's me and Sailor, Mama. We're riding with a friend."

His parents turned the porch light on, rushed to the car and grabbed Daughtry in a welcoming hug. "Where's your sister?"

"I'm here Mama," Sailor said, as she left the car to walk into the hug her parents offered.

"Come in, children and bring your friends. That includes the little furry one too, she said, patting Sam on the head.

"I'm so glad ya'll are here safe and sound. I've worried all day," Emilie said affectionately.

"Oh, Mama, you worry too much. Look at us, we're fine," Sailor chided.

"Fine my foot. I knew by your voice when you called earlier that something is going on. Get on in here and tell Mama what the problem is."

Sailor shrugged her shoulders and looked at her companions. "Mama's radar is working overtime. Nobody keeps secrets from Mama. She's the family Matriarch."

Frank chuckled. "I'm not surprised. You never can fool a woman, especially one as smart and pretty as you, Madam," he said, as he bowed with old school charm.

"Un hun! Now get in here before you all catch your death in the night air," she said as she sashayed back up the steps.

Emilie held the door open. She didn't miss the frightened look on Loren's face. It reminded her of a cornered animal. She noticed the quilt Loren was holding tightly against her body. Something was definitely amiss with this one she decided. She'd need to tread lightly or run the risk of speaking too soon.

"What a lovely quilt, Loren."

Loren swayed slightly. Emilie reached out to catch her arm, and her hand brushed against the quilt. Her eyes widened at the contact, but she pressed her lips together to keep from crying out. She let her hand drop to her side as the tingles continued to race up her arm. She flexed her fingers in hopes it would eliminate the strange sensation. It didn't. The tiny pinpoints of electricity were still there as she followed everyone into the house.

The smell of home-cooking permeated the interior of the house. Frank's stomach responded with a loud rumble as hunger recognized the smell of homemade gumbo. "Madam, I detect the unmistakable smell of a Louisiana specialty," he crooned.

"That is a yes . . . Mama's been cooking all afternoon. Soon as she heard the children were coming to town, the big pots came down, and they are simmering to the brim with all of Daughtry and Sailor's favorite foods," Maurice said.

Emilie looked at Loren. The child looked like she was ready to collapse. "Y'all head on into the kitchen. We'll be there in a minute," she said, with her eyes never leaving Loren's face.

Maurice caught the concerned tone of his wife's voice, and motioned for them to follow him.

When they left the room, Emilie led Loren to the sofa and gently pulled her down to sit beside her. She took her hands and held them on top of the quilt. "I don't know what is going on but something is happening here, child. I have a feeling this beautiful quilt you are holding may hold the answers to my questions."

"You feel the tingles?"

"Yes. Now, I need you to tell me why."

"It's the connection that our families share. Your ancestor, Alice, helped my ancestor, Georgiana, make this quilt during the Civil War. It guards a Promise. Someone wants to steal it."

Emilie squeezed Loren hands, and then ran her hands over the quilt excitedly. "Oh my Lord, I've heard rumors of this all my life. I never dreamed it was true! Do Daughtry, Sailor and Frank know about this too?"

"They know. It's why we're here. We have to hide it."

"Come on, child, let me put this quilt in a safe place so we can go into supper, and you can tell Mama all about it."

The bond of trust Loren felt with Emilie Corbin was sealed when she caught the reassuring scent of honeysuckle and rose in the air around her. She handed the quilt to Emilie, and watched her take a key from her apron pocket. She unlocked a wooden chest near the fireplace and placed the quilt inside. She locked the chest, held the key up for Loren to see, and smiled.

"Won't nobody be messin' with this tonight, unless you allow it?"

Loren followed her, pausing at the door to make sure she could see the chest from the kitchen. Satisfied that she could see if anyone came near the chest, she sat next to Sailor at the large table that was set with white stoneware bowls, spoons and red-checkered napkins.

It was quiet at the table until Maurice asked them to bow their heads so he could say grace. "Father in heaven, we are thankful for your love and protection. Be with us as we enjoy your bounty with friends and family. Amen"

As Emilie ladled gumbo into their bowls, she said, "Who wants to tell us what is going on here?"

Daughtry heard the determination in Mama's voice so he said, "it's Loren's story, Mama. She should begin it."

"Okay child, I'm listening."

As they enjoyed the rich flavor of the seafood and vegetable dish, Loren told Maurice and Emilie the story of the legend that had come into her hands after the death of her Gramma. She told them she believed fate had stepped in and led her to Daughtry and Sailor, who were connected to her family through Alice.

"This is wondrous. To think that our Alice, and your Georgiana, made that quilt that is out there in my chest. You don't know this, Loren, but that chest is the one Alice brought from Georgia with all her earthly belongings in it. There are some of her handmade handkerchiefs and small brooches in there. Also a hand-written letter and some of her books too. Lord she must have loved books. We always wondered how she'd learned to read. I bet your Georgiana taught her."

Loren smiled, "She did. I have Georgiana's journal. She wrote in there about secretly teaching Alice to read."

Emilie's eyes filled with tears. "She was so brave to teach a black child to read. Lord help us, if she'd been caught, it would have been awful."

She shuddered at the possibilities of what could have happened.

"Are you alright, Ms. Emilie?"

"Yes child, I'm fine. I was just thinking about some of the terrible happenings that our family passed down about the hardships of those days. Now, go on with your story."

Daughtry and Sailor kept their eyes on their Mama. They had heard some of the horrendous stories too; how the black children had suffered at the hands of cruel men. They knew there were many instances of kindness shown as well, but the horror that some chose to invoke on those in slavery was not easily forgotten.

When Loren mentioned the seeds, Daughtry shared what he had discovered after he had tested them at his laboratory.

Maurice's medical ears perked up and he interrupted. "Seeds, these seeds can heal!"

"Daddy, I know it sounds impossible, almost like a science fiction novel. Nevertheless, it's true. Grayson had leukemia, he touched the quilt that holds the seeds and now the leukemia is gone."

Maurice shook his head. "Son, what have you discovered?"

Frank butted in. "I'll tell you what it is. It's a miracle-working thing. Look at my Sam. He thinks he's a young pup now that he's touched that quilt. And me, well I've got a new lease on life. My old ticker hasn't worked this good in a decade."

Frank continued. "Seems like somebody other than us has found out about the seeds and they mean to have them. I figure the goons who were staking out Loren's

221

house last night went in to find the quilt, and when they came up empty, they headed back out here to report to their boss."

"Out here! You saying the people who are out to get the quilt are in Louisiana," Emilie said.

Daughtry looked at Sailor and shook his head. He didn't want her to blurt it all out in anger. After all, Jude was a friend of the family. They thought he was an upstanding pillar of the community.

Finally, trying to be as kind as he could, he said, "Daddy, Mama, the people that were watching Loren's house was driving a SUV that belongs to Jude Smith."

Emilie stilled, "Our Jude!"

"Yes, Mama, the car belongs to our Jude. It looks like he is the one bent on stealing Loren's heritage."

"Oh, Lordy . . . Lordy . . . I sense some trouble headed our way," Emily whispered.

Frank pushed his car back. He could see that the news that their friend was not who they believed him to be had shaken Emilie and Maurice.

"Madam that was a delicious meal and my stomach thanks you. I'm sorry we are the bearers of bad news, but your insight into our situation is dead-on. Trouble is brewing, and if I were a guessing man I'd say the pot is about ready to boil over. I believe it's time to get my buddy Colt Shaw over here. He's a U.S. Marshal that lives in the city. I gave him a call on the way here. He's been snooping around for me. Perhaps he has found out what your friend is intending to do."

"Yes, good idea, get him over here. We need to get to the bottom of this," Emilie said.

She walked to the living room, unlocked the chest and took the quilt in her arms. Loren watched her raise it to her face to inhale the fragrance. She knew what was happening. She had heard the quilt speak to her spirit too. God was at work arranging His plan. The circle of protectors were closing rank.

Loren walked from the kitchen to join Emilie. "You feel it, don't you? You know it has to be protected."

"With my life if needed," Emilie said, as she handed the quilt to Loren, and reached into the chest to get a beautiful hand-tatted handkerchief. She gave it to Loren. It was identical to the one that held the seeds that lay in the center of the quilt.

"Alice wrote that Georgiana had given her a handkerchief. They had made them to carry on Georgiana's wedding day. She said the handkerchief would be a reminder of the Legend of Promise that had bound them together. I never understood. Now I do," Emilie marveled.

The doorbell rang, breaking the silence of the moment. "That's Colton," Frank said as he rushed to open the door.

Twenty-Nine

Colton Shaw looked at the line-up of people staring at him when the door opened, and took a step back. Frank grabbed his arm, and leaned around him to look outside as if he was checking the place out.

"Alright, you've got my attention. What's going on," Colt asked.

As Frank pulled him forward, the crowd parted, and he found himself staring at a petite woman holding some kind of cloth covering. Her eyes held him captive. He vaguely heard Frank say, "We've got a situation that's brewing. My gut is telling me it's ready to blow. But, before we get to that, let's do some quick introductions."

Tearing his gaze away, he acknowledged the introductions, and heard Frank mentioned that Daughtry and Sailor had traveled from Tallahassee with him. Then he said, "This is Loren."

As he took a step forward with his hand extended, he could see the misty blue of her eyes. Red highlights that made Colton think of fireworks at a Fourth of July celebration, sparkled in her chestnut hair.

He felt her small hand slip into his. It was soft and warm against the roughness of his hand, as he covered it with his. He couldn't speak as the impact of her touch reached into the depths of his heart. She held his look and

225

smiled. Her smile reached in and melted places in his heart that he didn't realize were cold. He saw the awareness spark softly, as he squeezed her hand. The room was silent enough that he heard the sudden intake of her breath when her hand quivered in his. He caressed her palm in response.

Man what's going on here ran through his mind. Not wanting the moment to end, he started to reach for her, needing her to fill the emptiness that surrounded him as she withdrew her hand. His protective instincts pushed him to hold her, to tell her that no one would ever harm her as long as he was there to protect her.

Stepping back, Loren took a deep breath and encouraged her heartbeat to return to its normal rhythm before she dared to take another look at Colton. She really liked his lanky build that spoke of a disciplined athlete. His greenish-brown eyes and black hair cut close to his head would have looked feminine if the etched planes of his face, with its high cheek bones, had not been all male.

She tried to evaluate her sudden response to him. She wasn't a novice in the game of sexual awareness, but she had chosen to save her virginity for the man she would marry. This was new. He had broken through her defenses and she found herself longing to have him wrap his muscular arms around her, and never let go.

Sweet *Jesus, I need help*!

As soon as her frantic plea formed in her mind she breathed in the smell of honeysuckle and roses that swirled in the air between them.

226

You can trust this man. I've brought him here for you.

The spell was broken when Frank slapped Colton on the back and said, "Yeah, well, as I said, this is Loren. Like I told you on the phone we have reason to believe this guy, Jude Smith is after Loren's quilt."

Hearing Frank speaking, but still in a fog of emotions, Colton looked at him and mumbled, "Right, Jude Smith."

Frank laughed. "Come on, bud. Take a seat so we can give you the whole story. That is, if it's okay with Loren."

All eyes looked towards Loren, waiting for her to answer. The quietness surrounded her as she sat across the room from Colton. She needed to put distance between them so she could concentrate. She was still reeling from the impact of awareness that had literally taken her breath away, when he looked at her. He had gotten past her defense, and sparked something in her that no other male had ever achieved.

He was a virile man, the type she tended to shy away from. Her body responded to him, but at the same time her heart was telling her, he would keep her safe. Perhaps, it was because he was Frank's friend, or maybe, it was because he was an officer of the law. Whatever the reason, she knew he was person to be trusted, and that she would tell him what he needed to know.

Releasing a calming sigh, she looked at Colton and said, "Come sit with me. It's a long story, but you need to hear it all to understand why I must protect this quilt."

Colton took a seat in front of Loren. She smiled at him, and began her story. Colton listened. His eyes were drawn several times to the quilt. She stroked it as she talked. It seemed to him that she had a connection with it. When she voiced her concern about her parent's untimely deaths, he saw the hurt in her eyes and he assured her that he would see if he could find any current information that would let her have closure.

When she came to the part about finding Daughtry and Sailor, by following the feelings of her heart, he couldn't help but think her story sounded more like a fantasy than truth. In his line of work as a U.S. Marshal there wasn't room for finding people, simply by following your heart. He'd had the most success by pounding the pavement, until he found a lead that was good enough to close a case.

When Daughtry said the seeds in the quilt were unlike anything he'd ever seen, and that he didn't believe their origin was earth, Colton nearly laughed out loud.

"Not from earth. Where do you think they're from?"

Hearing the skeptical tone in Colton's voice, Daughtry cleared his throat and looked at him. "I believe they are from heaven. As Loren told you, the seeds were given to Pastor Smith by a beautiful angel. So, that's the only explanation that's possible."

"Hey, I believe you. Remember I live in a city where anything is accepted."

"No, please don't say that! They are from God!"

Her anguished cry sent a dagger of pain through his heart. He realized he'd hurt her. He leaned forward. "Loren, forgive me. I didn't mean to make such a stupid comment. I understand that you believe what you are telling me. But, I haven't been visited by an angel...or by God. I'm not saying he doesn't exist, but so far, He is just a name I've heard. I really don't know enough about Him to have an opinion."

Loren heard the words deep in her heart, *Show him who I am!*

Her tenseness melted as quickly as it had come. "It's alright, Colton," she said.

A puzzled look crossed his face. He turned his head, sniffing the air. "I smell roses...he sniffed again...and honeysuckle. Do y'all smell it?"

Loren leaned forward and said, "Colton, you can smell it!"

He felt his heart thud against his chest. His answer was lodged in his throat. He didn't have a clue what was happening, but he knew he was on the brink of something that just might have the ability to change his life forever.

Loren took his hands. She whispered, "Thank you Jesus" under her breath. Then she placed his hands on the quilt. The feel of the tingles made his hands tense but they stilled as Loren covered them with her hands. She knew what he was feeling.

"Now, let me tell you why this quilt is so important to me. Finding out about the legend my family has passed down is so much more than I can humanly understand. This quilt is precious to me because my ancestor, Georgiana made it. It symbolizes her undying love for Richard who was killed during the war. She didn't even have his body to bury. She never saw him again after he left. The quilt became a memorial to the love they shared. The morning Pastor Smith brought the seeds to her I believe she knew the perfect hiding place was the quilt. Each stitch she used to hide them was stitched with love. When the quilt was completed she used it to cover, Memorie, the child their love had created. I can see her tucking the quilt around their baby to surround her with her Daddy's love and with the gift from God. Colton, I can do no less than she and all the women in my family have done. The love Georgiana poured into the quilt has guided all of us for nearly two centuries. But, more than that, the Promise that God gave is still there, still guiding us. I will protect it whatever the cost. It represents the love of God and His Promise to mankind. According to the legend, there is healing in the seeds."

Colton shook his head. He wanted to believe, but he wasn't sure he could yet. Trying to be as gentle as he knew how to be he said, "I understand you believe this, Loren. I want to believe, but my life is directed by absolutes. There isn't room in my life for things I can't see or that don't have a logical explanation."

Loren lifted her hands to him, palm up. She was asking him to trust her. He looked at her fragile hands. He felt a tugging in his heart. He was drawn to Loren like a moth is drawn to a light. For the first time in his life, he needed another human being to feel whole. But, deep inside he realized it was more than her. Strange as it seemed to him, he heard a voice urging him to accept what she was offering. Could he really be hearing the voice of God the way Loren said she did?

He saw the question in her eyes. Without demanding an answer, she was compelling him to trust her. His mind battled. Did he dare to throw logic to the wind and trust this tiny woman and her God that drew him into their world?

Moments passed in silence. He looked at the people in the room. They didn't move or speak, just sat quietly, waiting for his answer.

Then he looked at Loren. She smiled, as if she knew a secret she wanted to share with him. The life he'd built so carefully was drifting farther away in his mind. He was driven to share whatever Loren was offering. He had to find out why she trusted a God that she'd never seen, and why she put so much importance in a simple quilt made of ordinary fabric.

In surrender, Colton placed his hands in hers. She laced her fingers with his and lowered their hands to touch the quilt again. His eyes never left hers, as they caressed the quilt. She watched the look of skepticism leave his face, as the dawn of acceptance replaced it. Colton saw the inner strength in Loren. He felt the flow of her strength, course through him.

"Colton, this is about more than us. We all have a destiny. Just as God led me to the people in this room, He has brought you here to be a part of His plan. He owns the entire universe and everything in it. That includes you and me. We are surrounded with His Presence and He is free to use everything to fulfill His purpose. He created everything that we can see, and He created all the things we cannot see. He is the beginning, and the end. His Word says if we don't praise Him the rocks will cry out in praise and adoration. Do you understand now why I must not let Him down? Why I must do what He has asked my family to do?"

Colton glanced at the people who were in the room. The storm raged outside, yet peace reigned inside. They all seemed to know where they fit into God's plan. Was it possible that Loren was right; that God had brought him here, to be part of a plan that had been set in motion centuries before any of them were born?

He wanted to believe he belonged, but it was so hard to let go of the barriers he built around his heart. He'd been a loner all of his life, never allowing anyone to get close. He couldn't understand why this time was different. Or how this lovely woman with her misty-blue eyes and a steadfast belief in her destiny had made him long for more than what he had.

As he caressed her hands with his thumbs, he realized it was one of the easiest decisions he'd ever made.

Whatever the next hours or days held, he would trust Loren's God and he would trust her. As wild as it still sounded to Colton, he chose to believe what Loren said. That God loved him and had a plan for his life. And that Georgiana's quilt connected their destiny's, bringing them together to carry out the will of God.

Thirty

Frank cleared his throat. "I can see you understand. It was hard for me to believe too. Wilder than any story I'd ever heard even during my years on the streets of New York City. Like I told you on the phone, Loren, Daughtry and Sailor showed up in my backyard before dawn this morning. They said someone was staking out Loren's house, it scared them and they made a get-away pronto. I believed them, first of all, because I knew Loren. I'd met the Doc at a couple of his speaking engagements, and I knew he had a reputation of being a square shooter. That belief was re-enforced when I saw the effect the quilt had on old Sam here and then on me. It's the real deal, and whoever is after it somehow must have learned what it can do."

"Yeah, pretty wild is a good description. Here's the thing. I could be missing something because of the short time I've had to work this. But, if I'm not, then everything I've found so far leads right back to Jude Smith."

Sailor whirled up from her chair. "That hypocrite! That Judas!

Daughtry stood. "Wait a minute. This doesn't make sense to me. We didn't know anything about this quilt until Loren came to us three days ago. How would he know?"

Emilie moaned, and everyone looked at her. "Lord in heaven, I think I might know how he found out!"

Maurice went to sit by her. "What are you saying, Emilie. You didn't know about it either."

She grabbed his hand and said, "I know but listen to me. Jude stopped by here about six months ago. Don't you remember, it was when you were doing the volunteer work at the shelter? He called and said he needed to ask me something. He had found some old papers that belonged to his Daddy. He had written about their ancestor, William Smith, who moved from Georgia to Louisiana right after the Civil War. He had moved here to be over the Children's Orphanage in New Orleans. Y'all know that our Alice moved with the Smith family to help at the orphanage."

"Mama, where are you going with this story," Sailor said impatiently.

"You just settle down, young lady. I'm getting there. Give me time."

"Do what your Mama said, Sailor. Go ahead, sweetheart, tell us why this has to do with Jude," Maurice encouraged.

"Well, like I said, he wanted to ask me a question."

Colton leaned close to her and said, "Ms. Emilie, what did he want to know?"

"He said his Daddy had written about remembering when he was a child that he'd heard his Daddy talk about a legend of some sort. He said it was passed down in the family that the colored girl, Alice, had helped her friend, Georgiana; hide something that had been given to his

236

Great-Granddaddy during the Civil War. He kept mumbling something about it rightfully belonging to him, and that he would have it, one way or the other."

"Emilie, why didn't you tell me about his visit?"

"Well, Maurice, I wasn't trying to hide anything from you. I didn't think any more about it. I told Jude that I had heard stories about a legend too, but there was never anything to prove that it was true. I bet he found out more than he was telling me. His Daddy must have had some proof that the legend really existed."

"You're right Mama. Jude must have figured this thing out. He knows who Loren is and that she has come to us," Daughtry added.

Frank looked at Colton. They stood.

"You're right. He knows Loren has the quilt and while he may not know the entire story, he knows enough to make him think it's worth his time to take it away from her," Frank declared.

"I'm so sorry, Ms. Emilie. He probably knows I'm here. I'm putting all of you in danger. It's just like my dream. I need to leave."

"Hush now, child. You are not going out in this storm. Besides, what are you talking about . . . what did you dream?"

Loren's face paled at the memory. "It was last night. I told Daughtry, Sailor and Mr. Frank about it. I have been so worried about the quilt; I thought that was why I had the nightmare. But now, with all that's happened, maybe it was a warning."

Emilie put her arm around Loren. "Sit down here and tell me what you dreamed. I believe God directs us through our dreams. Remember how Joseph, in the Bible, was called the 'dreamer'. God gave him dreams to guide him, so it stands to reason God will do the same for us too."

"You could be right, Ms. Emilie. But, it was horrible. Someone was chasing me, trying to take the quilt. I was running as fast as I could in the darkness, but they were gaining on me. I saw a light, and I knew I would be safe if I could reach it. I woke up before I made it to the light." Loren shuddered.

A loud crack of thunder pierced the night. Lightening zigzagged across the sky, illuminating the room as the rain hammered the metal roof. The siren of the wind pushed against the front door, threatening to blow it open.

Maurice said, "Listen to that racket outside. The storm is getting worse."

Emilie rubbed her hands on Loren's arms. "Well, I figure God must be telling us to stay put. You might think running away is a good plan but He must have a better plan for us."

Emilie glanced around the room and when she didn't hear any objections she said, "Okay, that settles it. We're not going anywhere tonight. A Louisiana storm is a sight to behold, and not something you want to take a ride in. I wouldn't want to be out there with the lightening popping and the ground getting soaked. Flash flooding is always a problem when we have this kind of rain. A dry highway can be underwater in minutes. Best thing I can think of is to get a good night's sleep and leave in the morning."

Frank ran his hand down the back of his head. "I agree with you, Emilie. We've got the danger from Jude Smith and the danger from the storm. We just need to decide which one we want to take on."

"Are you telling me Jude might show up here tonight?"

"I don't know, Maurice. If he is as desperate to get his hands on the quilt as I think he is, a thunderstorm certainly won't stop him."

"The weather isn't the only problem we have," Colt said.

Frank nodded. "Yeah, I've already thought about that. If he's figured out where we are, he'll have someone watching. Anyone leaving would have a tail following them."

"True, this guy grew up in New Orleans. He'll know the city like the back of his hand. We need a place that's not on his radar."

Maurice saw the look on Emilie's face. He knew the woman well enough to see that a light bulb has just turned on in her mind. "What are you thinking, darling?"

"I was thinking I know a place that would not be on Jude's radar."

"Yeah, how so, Emilie," Frank asked.

"We have a place in the outlying bayous. It's so deep in the woods the gators can't find it," she laughed.

"Mama everybody in the family knows where you and Daddy go to fish. In fact, Jude has been there with us," Daughtry commented.

"I'm not talking about the old family homestead, Daughtry."

"Mama, have you and Daddy got a secret hideaway," Sailor teased.

With a sparkle in her eye, Emilie said, "As a matter of fact, we do have a secret hideaway. We signed the closing papers on it yesterday, and as far as I know not a soul, other than the realtor, and us know where it is."

Frank caught sight of Loren's strained face. He watched her walk to the window to look out at the storm, and then pause at the front door. He could see that she was struggling with the guilt of putting others in danger. She looked worn out to him.

Turning back to Emilie he said, "Sounds like a good hideout. You ladies pack up the necessary essentials for an extended stay while we check the outside for the bad guys. If it's clear, we need to get out of here before daybreak."

"We can't," Emilie sighed.

"Why?"

"The road is nothing more than an overgrown one-lane road. It's passable when you can see in the daytime but with it storming and dark . . ." Her voice trailed off.

The tension in the room increased as Colton said, "Alright, we're back to square one. Daylight is not that far off so we'll wait for it. In the meantime, we'll stay put. Maurice, do you have any weapons in the house," he asked.

Sailor jumped up and cried, "Oh dear God, why do we need guns!"

Thirty-One

Her scared cry was cut short when the front door flew open. Jude Smith was framed against the furious darkness. Lightening bolted from the heavens, frying the soggy ground with a loud sizzle as he stepped inside.

Sailor shouted his name. There was silence, as everyone stood frozen by the anger shooting from Jude's glare.

Loren hugged the quilt closer to her chest. Colton carefully moved to her side and put his arm protectively around her waist. Jude glanced at her with arrogance. She didn't flinch under his scrutiny, just merely lifted her chin and returned his stare.

"Well, hello, Loren Taylor. I suppose an introduction is not necessary. I can see you already know who I am."

"Yes, I know who you are."

"That's good. You also know I have come for the quilt. I'm willing to pay top dollar . . . just name your price."

"It's not for sale."

"Right, you say it's not for sale, but we both know everything has a price – this is no different."

"The lady said it's not for sale. Do the smart thing by leaving and we'll forget you showed up here," Colton said.

Jude laughed. The sound was drowned out by the roar of thunder coming in through the open door.

Maurice stared at Jude. "Close the door, Jude. If you've got business here we can attend to it in a civilized way. Otherwise, you need to leave like Colton told you to."

Not bothering to close the door, Jude said, "Accept my apologies for involving you and Ms. Emilie in this, Maurice. If Loren had not slipped away in the night from Tallahassee, there would have been no need to follow her here."

"What is your involvement, as you call it Jude," Daughtry asked.

His face flushed in red-hot anger. He shouted, "My involvement is that the quilt is rightfully mine. I know the story from the papers Daddy left. He was too weak to take what is ours. He's dead, so I'm laying claim to the family treasure."

With a sinking feeling, Loren knew that he had found out about the seeds. He knew what they were capable of doing. She decided the best tactic was to face him without backing down.

"Who told you about the seeds?"

"It's all there in Daddy's handwriting. How some angel visited my ancestor, William Smith, in the middle of the Civil War to hand over three seeds that would be used to heal. He said he'd heard the story all his life, about Georgiana, and the black girl, Alice hiding the seeds for his Great-Granddaddy."

244

"If he knew the legend, why didn't your Daddy come after it," Loren asked.

Jude exploded. "I told you, he was too weak. He didn't have the guts to fight for what was his. He believed God was in control of the seeds. But, I'm not him. And, I don't need God telling me what I can or cannot do. I take what belongs to me!"

"It is not yours and you will not take it. If you really know the story, then you know that the pastor left it in the care of Georgiana. My family is the caretaker, not yours. I will not sell it to you, and I certainly will not give it to you."

Jude reached out as if he meant to grab the quilt. He drew his hand back; a look of shock crossed his features. The smell of honeysuckle and rose lightly drifted between them. She felt a surge of strength rise inside her. She thought about her Grandmothers, who had protected the quilt in times past. It felt as if they were surrounding her, protecting her, giving her courage.

God whispered. "Stand your ground, Loren!"

She held Jude's stare; never blinking as he looked at her with disdain. His voice rose in anger. "I don't know what funny stuff you just pulled, but it won't keep me from taking what is mine. Let's get real. I don't need, or want your God. Daddy said the seeds carry healing properties. I want them. I have the money and the power to use them. You're nothing – what can you do – you're just like the two women that hid them – powerless – without a clue what you have. Even if you did know the power of the seeds, you

245

are not smart enough to use it. I own the biggest pharmaceutical company in the state of Louisiana, with all the tools needed to mass produce your measly three seeds. I can turn them into millions of dollars, and control the world while I am doing it!"

Colton backed up to shield Loren as Jude stepped closer. Her dream flashed into her mind, and she heard a voice urging her . . . *run . . . run as fast as you can . . . do it now!*

She turned, and ran in the opposite direction, toward the back of the house. Jude's startled look was the last thing she saw before she heard the sound of flesh hitting flesh. She ran through the back door, out into the blackness of night that was made darker, by the blinding downpour of the storm.

Thirty-Two

The stunned look on Jude's face would have been comical under other circumstances, but at this moment, Colton didn't have time to enjoy it. Not thinking that Jude, in his fancy three-piece suit would be much of a challenge, he turned to see where Loren had gone. It was a mistake to turn his back on Jude. He felt the sucker punch to his kidneys; bringing him to his knees in pain.

Frank reached out to grab hold of Jude, but he pushed the older man out of his way. Maurice stood in the doorway, blocking him. "Where is your respect, Jude?"

"He doesn't know the meaning of respect, Daddy. If he did, he would not have come in here uninvited . . . or punched Colton. He's a Judas . . . He'll sell all of us to get what he wants," Sailor declared with utter contempt.

Jude raised his clenched fist, and took a menacing step towards Sailor, but he decided to back off when he saw Ms. Emilie coming his way. He was angry, but some little thread of conscience kept him from striking, Sailor or Ms. Emilie, who had treated him like a son after his Mama, died. He threw up his hands and said, "All of you be damned. The quilt is mine. I'll find Loren, and I'll make her pay for thinking she can escape."

With demonic anger contorting his face, Jude pushed his way past them, going out the back door. Turning

247

his head in every direction, he searched for sight of Loren. He didn't see her through the blinding rain. It was falling in dark sheets, driven sideways across the backyard by the howling wind.

"Frank, check out front, to make sure he came alone. We don't need his buddies piling in here unannounced."

"I'm on it. Go find Loren."

Colton heard Ms. Emilie cry out to God for protection as he ran to the open back door with his revolver drawn. He ran into the darkness, with the screech of the storm whipping him from side to side, ripping at the trees with all the fury of nature unleashed.

He felt like he had stepped into a black hole. He needed help, and he needed it fast, if he was going to protect Loren. That's when; Colton remembered the words that Loren had spoken less than an hour ago. She had told him that God was everywhere. Well, he didn't know if God listened to new believers, but he was going to find out.

With his eyes scanning the thick soup of the churning storm, Colton prayed as he ran, "God, I'm not used to this praying gig, but here goes. I need your help to find Loren."

In the next instant, lightning lit the sky, sweeping across the darkness like the beam of a lighthouse. Colton saw the shape of two people, struggling to stay upright as the storm battered their bodies. Loren was clinging to the quilt and fighting to stay on her feet as she stumbled in the darkness. Not more than ten steps behind her was Jude, who was gaining on her by the second.

"Thank you God," Colton shouted, as he followed the direction of the two people he'd seen for a moment. Without knowing it, he was taking the journey by faith because, now, everyone was shrouded in the blackness of night.

Thirty-Three

Loren gulped at the air, trying to keep oxygen in her lungs, as she ran in the pelting rain. It beat against her sensitive skin, soaking her, dragging her down into the muddy ground. She tried to hold the quilt above her head to keep it out of the mud as she fell, but the soggy quilt weighted her arms, and she fell headlong into a hole. She lay there, gasping for breath with her face buried in the quilt that was sinking in the rain-soaked ground.

My nightmare has come to life . . . help me, God!

She turned and heard Jude's voice carried on the wind. "You can't hide, Loren."

The sound of his heavy footsteps thundered across the yard. He was gaining on her. She had to run. She couldn't let him catch her. The darkness held her captive as she struggled to stand. She looked in every direction, crying out for God to show her a way of escape. Suddenly, a tiny pinpoint of light caught her attention in front of her. It spread out forming a circle that sparkled in the distance. *It looked like fireflies! Impossible . . . her rational mind shouted! It's storming . . . fireflies would not be in a storm!*

Gathering the quilt tightly in her arms, she started towards the light. When she took the first step, the rain stopped. An eerie quietness settled around her body, as she moved closer to the tiny circle of light that drew her.

Hope surged through her. She held the soggy quilt against her heart and ran as best she could towards the dancing lights. She stopped abruptly, when she realized her foot was on the edge of a bayou. She could not run any further. She was trapped.

"Oh God, No! What can I do now?"

"God will not help you, Loren. It's the end of the road for you. Give me the quilt," Jude choked out angrily.

She slowly turned to see Jude standing behind her. He was breathing heavily, and was pointing a revolver at her. She saw his hand jerk as he pressed his finger against the trigger of the gun.

Colton was standing behind Jude, with his gun pointed at Jude's back. He knew it might be a useless gesture, but, perhaps he'd be fast enough to get the first shot if Jude wasn't bluffing.

"Step away from the water, Loren," Colton said.

Jude threw his head back and laughed, "Go ahead, big man. Shoot me and the bullet will get her too."

The challenge hung in the stillness.

Throw it towards the light, Loren!

She heard God, but her heart argued with his wisdom. *What are you asking me to do? I have to protect the quilt! I can't throw it away! Please, God find another way.*

Trust me, Loren. Throw it towards the light!

With a heartbreaking wail, Loren whirled away from Jude. She lifted the rain-soaked quilt as best she could, and threw it with all her might. The quilt had barely left her hands when the wind billowed under it, lifting it on the currents, carrying it towards the dark water of the bayou.

"No, you stupid idiot, it's mine," Jude shouted. He pushed her to the ground, and lunged to grab the airborne quilt.

With Jude out of his way, Colton reached for Loren. He pulled her away from the water's edge, wrapping his arms tightly around her. Drawing her back against his body, they watched Jude plunging deeper into the dark water. He threw the gun down, and was frantically grabbing for the quilt, as it was carried further into the bayou by the wind.

"You stupid woman! I'll make you pay for your foolishness," he ranted, like a maniac, as he moved farther into the water, trying to grab the elusive quilt.

Colton and Loren saw him stumble; go under the water and surface again as he went deeper and deeper into the bayou. The water rose to his waist as he made a final desperate grab at the quilt that had settled on the surface of the water in front of him. His hand caught the edge of it.

He turned to look at Loren and Colton. She shuddered when she saw the gleam of madness in his eyes. His dark face looked like a person who was tottering on the rim of insanity to her, as he chanted, "I won! You lost! I have it! I told you it's mine!"

He hung on to the quilt, slowly pulling the soggy fabric to his body.

Jude's sing-song voice echoed across the water as he started back to the shore. A movement above his head caught Colton and Loren's attention. They saw a dark cloud gather above Jude, as if it was drawn together by an unseen hand. A bolt of lightning shot from the cloud to stab the spot in the water where Jude was. They knew he never saw it coming.

He cried out as it pierced his body, pinning him to the quilt. He was still holding onto it, as it entombed his body that had become a mass of burned flesh. A moment later, Jude and the quilt were gone.

Loren started to hide her face, wanting to block out what she'd seen. She hesitated, to watch a brilliant light form above the spot where they'd seen Jude and the quilt disappear. It was radiant white. In the midst of the light, Loren and Colton saw an angel. He looked at them, and smiled. The love from his smile streamed across the water, covering their bodies in heavenly warmth. It filled their hearts and minds, blocking out the horror of what they had just witnessed. They stood there, speechless, as the angel's magnificent eyes comforted them for a split second longer, and then he was gone.

"Colton, did you see him?" Loren whispered.

Shaken to his toes and begging his rational mind to click in, Colton said, "It depends on what you're talking about."

"I'm asking you if you saw the bright light and the angel smiling at us."

He shook his head. "Yeah, that's what I saw. I've never seen anything like it in my life."

Colton drew her closer and cradled her against his chest. She raised her arms to clasp her hands above his head. They stood in silence, shielding each other, trying to understand all that had happened. They felt suspended in time. They knew they needed to let the others know what had happened, but they were unable to move.

The lull in the storm was over as the rain fell. Loren heard Colton say, "We need to get back to the house."

"Oh God, Colton, Jude's dead isn't he?"

Holding her close, Colton felt Loren tremble when he whispered, "I don't know, Loren. We need to get help."

Taking ragged breaths, she slipped her hand in his and pulled him to the edge of the bayou with her. When she spoke, Colton thought it was the saddest sound he had ever heard. "Georgiana's quilt is gone. God told me to throw it towards the light. I did what He said, but it hurts so badly. I don't understand why He'd tell me to throw the Promise away," she sobbed.

He held her as tears ran down her cheeks. There was no need for words. Words could not erase her decision. Grief from the loss shook her body. He rubbed her back, offering whatever comfort he could.

The bright beam of flashlights found them. They heard Frank shout, "Colton, where are you boy?"

"Over here, by the bayou, Frank."

Daughtry, Frank and Maurice walked towards them holding umbrellas above their heads. Maurice handed one to Colton. He opened it and drew Loren under it with him. He circled her with his arm, holding her close.

Frank noticed the look of shock on Loren's face in the dim light. He pointed the flashlight beam towards the edge of the water and said, "Where's Jude?"

Colton pointed to the bayou. "Lightening got him. He went in after the quilt."

The questions could be seen in the three men's eyes but Colton's slight nod towards Loren was enough to keep them silent.

"Come on, Loren; we need to get out of this rain."

She didn't move. She looked back at the bayou. Pleading for him to understand, Loren said, "I can't leave the quilt. Maybe it's not really gone. It might still be there in the water? Surely God wouldn't destroy it. I have to find it."

Her soft voice tugged at his heart. He caressed her arms. "Loren, it's too dark right now for us to find it. We'll come back as soon as it's daylight. I promise."

Holding her hand, and drawing her under the umbrella, Colton walked with her towards the house where Emilie was waiting at the door. When she saw Loren, she gathered her close against her bosom, holding her trembling body, crying with Loren as she told her that Jude had tried to get to the quilt and was struck by the lightening.

"It's gone. It's lost in the dark water of the bayou along with Jude."

Sailor gasped as she heard Loren say Jude was gone. "Gone? Is he dead?"

Maurice put his arm around Sailor and said, "Let's all go inside. We need to call 911."

Colton dialed the number, and gave the dispatcher the necessary information. After the call, he looked at each of them before he spoke. "We need to decide on our part of the story before the authorities arrive. Jude is well known in the city so his death will be front-page news by tomorrow."

Emilie spoke. "What do you mean . . . decide on our part of the story?"

Loren spoke first. Her voice was shaky but firm in its conviction. "Colton, we can't tell anyone about the legend!"

"That's why we need to get our story together. I have an idea. Things can be hidden in plain sight. I'm not asking you to tell anyone about the legend, but maybe the quilt can be used as the reason for the accident."

"Sit down everybody. Colton, you and Loren are soaking wet. Go put dry clothes on while I get coffee perking," Emilie said.

"There's not enough time for us to change, Ms. Emilie. The sheriff will be here in minutes. Everybody listen, this is our story. It's not a secret that southern people are known to be overly-obsessive about family heirlooms. We'll say the quilt caused a dispute between Loren and Jude, when he decided his family should have inherited it. When he came here tonight to claim the quilt, Loren panicked, and ran into the storm. Jude followed her and accidently ran into the water, and was struck by lightning."

257

Frank pondered the story. "Colton's right. Those goons who followed Loren to Tallahassee would know about the quilt, but I doubt Jude had told them about the seeds."

Colton saw the uncertainty in Loren's face. He sat next to her, pulling her close to him. "Loren, you told me that God can do anything. We have to trust Him."

"Colton, that is amazing. You are a new believer, but yet you trust God completely."

"Alright, that's the story we'll give the sheriff. Now, we need to hear the real story before they arrive," Frank said.

"I can tell you this, Frank; Jude's death was not an accident. The lightning that hit him came out of nowhere. The sky had cleared, but when he went in the water after Loren's quilt, a single bolt nailed him."

Emilie shuddered. She remembered the tingles she'd felt when she touched the quilt. She thought about the man who had touched the Ark of the Covenant in the Bible and was struck dead. It made her more certain than ever that the quilt was set aside for God's use.

What she couldn't understand was why God would destroy it. If the seeds were to be used for healing, and they were gone, how could their purpose ever be fulfilled?

Her thoughts were interrupted as they heard the wail of sirens. Emergency Services were here. Maurice went to open the door. Sheriff Harris, a deputy and the paramedic came inside. The sheriff spoke to Colton, who had come with Maurice to the door. They had worked on several

258

cases in and round New Orleans over the years and had a lot of respect for each other.

Sheriff Harris said hello to them, and listened to Colton as he gave a brief account of what had happened. If he wondered why a U.S. Marshal was involved in the accident, he didn't voice his opinion. When Colton finished his story, all the men walked down to the bayou with the sheriff.

Loren, Sailor and Emilie watched them go. They joined hands. "Oh, Lord, I hope they find Jude's body. He doesn't have any close family living. It'll be up to us to take care of the arrangements." Loren and Sailor squeezed Emilie's hands, seeking to comfort her. They knew today was going to be a stressful day.

Thirty-Four

The rain had stopped completely, and daylight had arrived by the time Sheriff Harris came back to the house. He told them the Medical Examiner and the dive team were there to recover the body.

"I'd rather you all stay inside until we get this taken care of. In the meantime, I need to get your statements."

Emilie invited him to have a cup of coffee, while Colton and Loren put on dry clothes. When they were all seated in the kitchen, Colton made sure that Loren was seated near him. Her face was pale, and her voice shaky, as she told the Sheriff that Jude had frightened her, when he demanded that she give her family quilt to him.

"I panicked and ran. He followed me!"

Sheriff Harris looked at her, clearly seeing the distress mirrored on her face.

"The quilt fell into the bayou and Jude went in after it. The lightning struck him. It was horrible." Loren shuddered

"Did anyone else see what happened?"

"I did Sheriff Harris," Colton said.

He looked at the sheriff without blinking an eye. "It happened just like Loren said."

The sheriff held his gaze a moment longer and said, "I understand, Loren. Family treasures are important. I'm sorry you had to witness this tragedy. I need you folks to stay in Mandeville a couple of days. By then the body should be recovered and we can get an all-clear for you all to go home."

"We're not going anywhere, sheriff. As for Loren, I've already told her she needs to rest up before she goes back to Tallahassee. The child has had more than her share of upset." Emilie said.

With goodbyes said, and everyone seated around the table, Emilie gathered the ingredients to prepare omelets for a late breakfast. While she measured, chopped and stirred the ingredients to get it ready for the hot grill, they sat in silence, watching her. Maurice knew the busy-work was her way of handling the death of Jude. Even though he had proven himself to be less than a friend to the family, they couldn't help but mourn his passing in respect of their family's long-time acquaintance.

"Charles would turn over in his grave if he knew what his son did."

Sailor put her arms around him. "I'm so sorry, Daddy. I know you and Jude's daddy were best friends."

"Yes we were. He was a fine man. We grew up together right here in Mandeville. That's why we have to protect their family name from being slandered. Just because Jude turned out to be a bad seed, we can't let the press crucify the Smith family name in the news."

"There's no way to keep it out of the news, Maurice. Like Sheriff Harris said, Jude is well-known in Louisiana, so this will be a headline story for local and national news. He was wealthy, and for the most part well-respected. Only those who'd bothered to look beyond the

262

dollar signs, knew the face he presented to the public was not the only face he had. The Food and Drug Administration (FDA) was closer than ever to making a case against him for skimming regulations at his pharmaceutical facility. He'd been short changing the consumer for years with his shoddy business dealings. If that information leaks out, the press will have enough to chew on for weeks. That could be the nugget that takes the attention off of the accident, and lets Loren's involvement slide by unnoticed," Colton said.

Loren sighed. "I am so sorry . . . I didn't mean to bring this on your family, Mr. Maurice."

"You hush now, child. You are part of this family, because of Georgiana and Alice. Furthermore, you didn't bring this tragedy to our home; Jude did that when he chose to follow his greed above his good family name," Emilie said as she served up the delicious egg omelets.

Frank patted her shoulder in concern. "Colton said it was pretty bad out there. But, you'll be okay. We're all in this together."

"I'm afraid it won't ever be okay for me. I lost the quilt, Mr. Frank."

"I know. Colt said you did what was best. After we eat, some of us can go down there and see if the divers found it."

"Mama, you are the best cook in the world," Sailor blurted out, attempting to take Loren's mind off of her loss.

"Yes, I am. And to prove it, I want every one of you to clean those plates by eating every bite."

They finished the meal, making small-talk about the finicky weather in Louisiana. As if to prove their point, the bright rays of the morning sun sparkled through the window panes. Rainbow colors danced off the kitchen appliances.

"Look at that, Loren, its God's rainbow promise. Every time I see a rainbow, it reminds me that God is in control of the circumstances in this old world."

The corners of Loren's mouth turned up in a smile. "That's what Gramma Lil always told me, Ms. Emilie. Thank you for reminding me. I needed to hear those words of wisdom this morning."

They heard a knock on the door. Everyone's head turned at the same time to see Sheriff Harris standing there.

"Come in, sheriff," Emilie said

"Thank you, Ms. Emilie."

He opened the screen door, walked in and stood there a moment before he said, "The divers are still looking for the body. The bayou is all-churned up from the storm last night. The silt from the bottom is making it nearly impossible to see a foot ahead of you. I wanted to let you know that we are going to continue the search throughout the day, but chances are the body was washed out to the gulf during the storm."

Maurice stood. He cleared his throat. "Okay, thank you sheriff. Our family appreciates that. I know that you are doing all that's possible to find Jude."

Loren reached for Colton's hand. She held it tightly, the unshed tears burning her eyes. "Did you find my quilt, sheriff?"

"No, mam. I'm sorry. We haven't found anything. Not the body or the quilt. It doesn't seem like there is anything there at all."

Colton felt her hand tremble in his. His heart pounded in his chest. He hurt for her loss but he felt powerless to help her. As he struggled with his need to be there for her, he silently prayed, *God Loren needs you, please ease her pain.*

Thirty-Five

The rest of the day was spent listening to the sound of voices from the bayou, as the recovery team criss-crossed the dark water, searching for Jude's body. The clank of the heavy chain, when it was pulled tight as it snagged something on the bottom, meant a diver would enter the water to see what had been found.

Emilie, Loren and Sailor, had gone to town to get away from the sounds and sights of the gruesome search. The men had sat on the back porch of the house, talking about their different adventures in their chosen professions. They made numerous trips to the water's edge, to see if there was any news of a recovery. They had watched the reporters snapping photos of the divers, and pushing microphones at the sheriff, hoping to get a story.

One of the more enterprising of the reporters decided to visit the Corbin's house, but he was stopped halfway up the hill by Daughtry. Maurice was impressed with his son's ability to handle the press. He overheard Daughtry tell the reporter that he was barking up the wrong tree, by infringing on a family's grief. The reporter took the hint, and headed back to the bayou where the sheriff was giving a statement.

"It's the waiting that gets you," Frank said.

"Yeah, the waiting is what wears you out. But, there's not a thing you can do to hurry the process along," Colton agreed.

267

They heard the front door open, and Emilie called out that they were home. She came into the kitchen, her arms loaded with grocery bags.

Maurice rushed to help her. "Let me have that, Emilie. Looks like you tried to buy the store out," he teased.

"Daddy, you've been saying that ever since I was a child," Sailor said with a girlish giggle.

The affection for her parents could be seen by those watching. It tugged at Loren's heart, making her miss the Mama she couldn't really remember, and even more, it made her lonesome for Gramma.

"Gramma used to say the same thing ever time we went shopping. When I was a teenager, I thought she was complaining about the cost of providing for me. Later, I realized it was her way of including me."

Emilie patted her arm with affection. "I can see that your Gramma loved you, Loren. You are a fine young woman, one that any parent would be proud to call their own."

Frank had watched the expression on Colton's face as the women talked about family. He could see the struggle, and knew that Colton had fought the demons of abandonment, from childhood. It had begun long before he was taken from his abusive family, at the age of four.

From what little Colton had said the series of foster homes he'd been placed in, were not much of an improvement from where he'd started out in life. He'd told Frank, most of the foster parents were good people, but they usually had so many kids coming and going in the system, that they didn't have time to form lasting bonds with any of the children.

When they had been partners, working the streets of New York City, Frank had asked him why he chosen law enforcement as a career. He'd never forgotten Colton's answer. He'd said when he was around twelve years old; he'd been out on the street one night, wondering if there was anyone in the world, who could love him. An older cop had taken the time to sit with him on the park bench, for nearly an hour. He'd seemed genuinely interested in Colton, and what he wanted to do with his life. It was the first time anyone had taken the time to be a role-model in his life. *That's why I do what I do, Colton had said. I wanted to make a difference in people's life, the same way he had made a difference in mine.*

Frank drew his thoughts back from the past when he heard Sailor say that she and Loren were cooking tonight.

"You all go find something to do. We need space in the kitchen to create our masterpiece."

Daughtry chuckled. "Mama, need I remind you of the last time Sailor set out to create a masterpiece?"

Emilie hushed him with her upheld hand. "Let the girls alone, Daughtry. Perhaps Loren is a better cook than your sister."

Maurice, Frank, Colton and Loren listened to the easy banter as the siblings' poked fun at each other. The sad look had disappeared from Colton's face as he smiled, and hugged Loren close. Her misty blue eyes sparkled,

269

reminding him of the Caribbean Sea on a clear day. Warm .
. . inviting. A place you didn't want to leave.

She looked up at his smile. Warm spread up her
body and wrapped around her senses. Looking into his
commanding eyes, she felt the force of his attraction
drawing her in. She was almost undone when he said, "I'll
eat whatever you fix, and enjoy every bite."

The look of open adoration on his face as he held
Loren was so obvious that Frank nearly shouted . . . *oh man
. . . love is in the air!* He turned to the others standing there
who were watching the exchange just like he was.

Loren eased out of Colton's embrace. Her cheeks
were tinged in a bright red of embarrassment as she
realized the intimate moment had been visible to everyone
in the room. She sent up a silent prayer for strength to resist
such a glaring temptation. She was determined not to end
up paying with her heart if she let herself make the wrong
choice.

Colton felt bereft as he watched her back away. She
held his gaze and he couldn't help but appreciate her
feminine curves, her long legs, trim ankles and dainty
toenails, painted a pale pink. His heartbeat pounded in his
ears.

*Whoa! Put the brakes on before you make a fool of
yourself.*

Sailor clapped her hands loudly, and told everyone
to leave the kitchen. "Don't enter this room until I give the
okay."

"Okay, guys, that's our cue to clear out," Maurice said candidly.

Taking the lead, Frank led them out the back door. The afternoon was quickly being given up to the shadows of night. From where they stood, they saw that the rescue boat was at a standstill in the water. The divers had shed their gear and were packing up their equipment.

"They must be calling the search off."

"Yeah, looks that way to me too. Let's head down there and see what's going on," Colton said.

Sheriff Harris saw them and walked towards them. "We're packing up. There's nothing in this bayou except fish and bullfrogs. I figure the body has drifted. We'll check downriver at first light tomorrow, but I'll be truthful. I don't figure we'll make a recovery."

The men stayed until the boat was loaded and the last vehicles had driven away. They watched the tail-lights disappear in the gathering darkness, and then turned to the bayou that was as peaceful as a baby's contented sleep.

Maurice spoke what they were all wondering when he said, "Loren will be heartbroken when she hears they didn't find her quilt."

No one thought it strange that his mind was more concerned with the loss of the quilt than the loss of a traitor.

Thirty-Six

The strain of the day settled in Loren's neck as she chopped greens for the salad they were serving, along with Sailor's pot of spaghetti. The aroma drifted around her, as she listened to the off-key sound of Sailor singing the latest commercial ditties, while she stirred the fragrant sauce bubbling on the stove.

The peaceful scene was not enough to erase the awful memories of the past twenty-four hours from Loren's mind. But, even with the horrendous details of Jude's betrayal and death, she found comfort in the way God had led her to the Corbin family. The wonder of His direction that had connected her with them after centuries was proof in her mind that she served a loving God, who was involved in the details of His children.

Her heart picked up speed, as she thought about meeting Colton. She liked everything about him. He was intelligent, and had shown he had a sense of humor, but it was the feeling of safeness that she felt when he was near that spoke the loudest to her. He was like an oasis in a desert that brought a promise of a new beginning.

The door swung open, startling her back to the present, as the object of her thoughts came into the kitchen. Each time she saw him, his appeal was stronger, more compelling, and robbed her of reasonable thought.

"Hi . . . ," he crooned as he took in every inch of her. He loved her beauty that was more than an outward façade. Her inner beauty shined brightly, even though she had suffered in the last hours. Her strength of character was enormous in the face of all that had happened.

Slow down, old man. The lady has to have a few flaws.

She cleared her throat; her face flushed red as if she'd heard him speak his thoughts out loud. "Hey, did they find anything?"

Colton took her hands. "Come set with me at the table."

Maurice, Daughtry and Frank came in as she asked the question. He told her the sheriff had called the search for Jude off until tomorrow.

"He has to be there. We saw him go into the water. We saw the lightening strike him. They should find him."

"Loren, they might not. The lightening could have destroyed his body. If it didn't, the Sheriff thinks it could have drifted."

"Oh my God, that is horrible. Please tell me they at least found the quilt."

Colton shook his head. Loren looked at him and the look of pain he saw mirrored on her face felt like a kick to his gut. He was helpless to take away her pain, and it gnawed at him.

Maurice spoke softly. "Loren, it's too dark now, but when morning comes we'll go take another look. Perhaps it is lodged against the cypress knees along the edge. We'll find it, I promise."

He was right. Where was her faith? This was God's journey. He was in control.

"You're right, Mr. Maurice. We'll look tomorrow. I'm sure it will be there."

Emilie came into the kitchen, bragging about the delicious smell that had drawn her there. Sailor loved hearing Mama's words of approval. She was a grown woman with a career, but she loved pleasing her parents. With all the dignity of a hostess at a high priced establishment, she told the family to have a seat and she would serve up the promised feast.

They enjoyed the food, and Sailor beamed at their compliments. "It's an improvement from the last time. Loren is a good influence on your culinary skills," Daughtry said with a straight face.

She thumped him on the top of his head. When he started to return the same in her direction, Maurice said, "No fighting at the table."

Laughing at the parental reprimand that helped to lighten the solemn mood that hung over the supper table, they spent the rest of the meal not talking about the day's events. It seemed to help, even though they knew it was still there, and would need to be dealt with.

After supper, Colton pushed back his chair and excused himself. He told them he needed to check in with his office. Loren stood and said, "I'll walk you to your car."

He took her hand as they walked out. The moon hung low on the horizon. It created a peaceful ending to a horrible day that had been filled with unthinkable chaos.

They walked slowly, hands swinging between them, each of them wanting to delay their parting. Colton opened the truck door and turned back to embrace Loren. Words were forgotten as he laid his cheek against her hair. The faint smell of coconut from her shampoo made him think of a tropical paradise. The thought of them lying on a sunny beach made his gut tighten. He felt her response.

He cradled her face in his hands, taking his time, filling the moment with tenderness that melted her heart. "Aw, sweet Loren, something is happening here. I know we've just met, but, to me it feels . . . it feels like being in the sun after you've been stuck in the grey, damp shade forever."

The care and tenderness he showed toward her, made her ache with longing. Her mouth went dry. She swallowed. Colton caressed her cheek.

"Is it possible to feel this deeply about someone you've just met?"

"You tell me, Loren. I can only speak for myself, and I can't imagine a day without you in my life."

His tender expression captivated her. "When this is all over, will you go out to dinner with me?"

"I would love to go to dinner with you."

He gently traced the curve of her cheek. "That's what I was hoping you'd say."

She stood back as he got in the truck, and drove away. Her awareness of him as a man, was working overtime. At the same time she could see the dramatic change in his attitude, and understanding of God. Gramma had told her numerous times that God had the perfect mate for each of us, if we were willing to wait on His timing. She said they would complete each other, physically, intellectually, emotionally and spiritually.

Could Colton be the one you've chosen for me? Could it happen this fast!

As the questions bombarded her mind, she decided she needed to find a quiet spot to talk with God.

She opened the door, and heard the soft rumble of the family talking in the kitchen. The desire to slip away, fought with the need to let them know where she was. She joined them.

"Loren, sweetheart, sit down and I'll get you something to drink," Emilie said.

"Thanks, Ms. Emilie, I'm fine," she said, taking a seat near Sailor.

"We were discussing our plans, Loren. Even if Jude is not found, Daddy said we need to have some sort of memorial for him. People would expect us to do that."

Loren shuddered as she remembered the last time she'd seen Jude. She did not want to see him again.

Sailor slipped her arm around her and said, "We don't expect you to attend, Loren. After what he did, I don't want to either, but we've got to do what is expected of us."

Emilie rose. "Enough talk about this. I am exhausted. Frank you can use Daughtrys' room and he will sleep in the den. I'll take Loren to the guest room."

"I appreciate your hospitality, Emilie, but Colton is expecting me to stay with him. He's got a month off, doctor's orders after his tangle with that hotshot that punched him in the kidney. We need to plan a relaxing fishing trip, to help him with his healing process," Frank joked.

"Well, we'll see you tomorrow. Maurice lock up, me and the girls are calling it a night," Emilie said, as she followed Sailor and Loren out of the kitchen.

Thirty-Seven

The faint moonlight shimmered through the wooden slats of the windows. It danced across the green satin comforter that Loren had pulled up to her chest. She traced the pattern with her fingertips, and quietly talked with God. The fear that had tried to overtake her when Jude had chased her was laid to rest. She didn't know if anyone else had knowledge of the quilt, but that really didn't matter now. The quilt was gone. She closed her eyes in an effort to stop the tears that wanted to flow.

"God, my heart is heavy. I did what I heard you tell me to do. I threw the quilt into the light. I trust your wisdom, even though the quilt is gone. But, that doesn't keep me from missing it. When I think about never seeing it or holding it in my arms, I grieve. Please help me to get pass the hurt."

She knew that God was not surprised by the way things had unfolded, but somehow she felt responsible. Oh, she knew that was silly thinking. God was capable of handling anything, and He certainly didn't need her help in making things turn out a certain way, but still - she wished she could have done more.

"God, please take away the feeling of hopelessness. Let me feel your peace in my heart. And, help the Corbin family to get through the things they are facing because of

Jude's actions. Most of all, thank you for bringing these special people into my life."

In her mind she pictured Colton's face. His rugged face was framed with midnight hair that made her fingers itch to touch it. His compassionate eyes and easy smile had been an anchor for her today. She smiled at the memory of the way he had touched her. He made her feel like she was precious. Like someone to be valued.

Before she said amen she whispered, "God, thank you for Colton. He saved my life last night. I feel gratitude for that but; the fact is I am feeling a lot more than just gratitude. Guide my decisions concerning these feelings, in Jesus Name, I pray."

The peace spread through Loren and she slept. The household had been in full swing long before she opened her eyes to the sun welcoming her to a new day.

. . .

She sat up, glanced at the clock and was shocked to see the hands were pointing to ten o'clock.

"Good Lord, I'm a sleepy-head. But, thank you. You knew what I needed," she said as she lifted her hands to heaven.

Fifteen minutes later she followed the voices to the back porch. Sailor and her mama were in the porch swing, eating cereal and touching their toes in unison to make the swing glide smoothly. She sat in a rocker at the other end of the porch.

"I didn't mean to oversleep, Ms. Emilie," she apologized.

"Hush, child. We just got up too. It's a beautiful day and we wanted to enjoy it. It's amazing how God can wash the earth with the rains of a storm and then send the sun to dry it the next day. Go get you a bowl of cereal and come back out."

Loren did as she was told. She sat, drawing her bare feet under her as she munched the crispy cereal. She could see Maurice, Frank and Daughtry as they slowly walked towards the house, deep in conversation.

Colton had promised to walk with her to the bayou later. He said he had a small pirogue that he could paddle around the bayou to see if the quilt had gotten tangled in the cypress knees along the edges of the shore.

Maurice told them the area was clear. The sheriff had called earlier to let them know they would continue the search down-river for Jude until nightfall.

"He didn't sound very hopeful of recovering his body."

"Poor old Jude. Bless his heart, what a horrible end to such a promising life," Emilie said.

No one commented. There wasn't anything they could say, to change the outcome. He had made his choice in life, and suffered the consequences. That was how God had designed human behavior. Each action carries a reaction. Jude's desire for power through greed had cost him his life.

Frank spoke into the silence. "Colton said he will be over later. He wants to nose around to see if the two guys who found Loren in Tallahassee are clean. Chances are, it will be hard to prove anything if he does find them. He said Jude was extra careful in who he used to do his dirty work."

Emilie left them on the porch. She said she needed to look after some chores since friends and family were sure to come by, as soon as the news about Jude was known. Sailor went with her. Maurice and Daughtry went inside too, Maurice to check on possible arrangements for a memorial, and Daughtry to call his answering service in Tallahassee.

Loren glanced up at the cloud-dotted sky. "Thank you for all you've done for me, Mr. Frank."

"You very welcome, Loren. Thank you for all you've done in my life too. God was a distant question in my mind. Now, He is the one with all the answers. You have given me a new lease on life, with more purpose that I've had in decades."

"He doesn't want to be distant from His children. The Bible says that He is the perfect Father, loving His children, and always wanting the very best for us."

Frank looked at her with kindness. "I know you are right, Loren, but yet, we lost the quilt that held His Promise to mankind. How can that be the best thing?"

The question hung between them. Loren wanted to give the right answer to encourage Mr. Frank to trust God, even when her faith was shaken. She decided to be totally honest.

"I don't know why God allowed the quilt to be lost. I may never understand why. One thing I do know is that

God is still in control. He doesn't need a quilt, made by human hands, to protect what He created. I believe the reason He sent the seeds to earth, was so that we could be a part of His plan. Gramma Lil always said that every time God sent a soul from heaven in human babies, it was so we could share in what He had created in heaven. Sometimes we're not allowed to keep those children here forever. Maybe, God decided to take the Promise back to heaven."

A blush like a shadow crossed over her pale complexion. "I don't mean to preach."

Frank shook his head. "That's not preaching, Loren. That's sharing your belief. It's good. I want to hear more about your faith in God."

She stood up. "Anytime, I love to talk about Him. He is my dearest friend. Now, I'll go see if Ms. Emilie needs my help."

"That's good, Loren. I'll wait here for Colton. He should be here soon."

Frank watched her until she closed the door. He was struck again by the strength she showed in the face of adversity. She had been battered by life from the time she was a toddler, yet she continued to pull herself up, to face whatever came at her. She didn't seem to know the meaning of giving up. He prayed to have faith like this small woman who had taught him more about God in the last forty-eight hours, than he'd heard in his entire life.

Frank chuckled. He thought about the commercial that touts a bunny that keeps on going. He figured Loren ought to apply for the job, she was certainly qualified.

His musing was interrupted by Colton, when he opened the screened door. The look on his face made Frank's law instincts kick up a notch. He pointed to a rocker for Colton to sit in and asked, "What did you find out?"

"Just like we figured it would happen. They skipped out of town. I threw a few questions out on the street, but anyone that might know something about their location has clammed up."

"I don't care where they are, as long as they stay away from the Corbin's and Loren," Frank said.

"New Orleans P.D. will flush them out once this story on Jude's underhanded business practices surfaces. Until then I imagine they will choose to lay low."

"Yeah, that sounds about right. I was thinking, since you're on vacation you might want to drive me and Loren to Tallahassee. Daughtry and Sailor will want to stay for the memorial. I can leave them my buddy's car to drive back, when they're ready to come home."

The kitchen door opened. His stomach clenched at the sight of Loren standing in the doorway. She wore blue Bermuda shorts with a matching flowery top that showed off her slender arms and graceful neck. Her rich brown hair shimmered in the afternoon sun, turning the red highlights into streaks of fire.

In her hands, she carried a white leather book with tiny embossed flowers. It looked very old. The picture she made reminded him of priceless paintings created by the master artist of long ago. She really was lovely, with natural beauty that she didn't cover behind layers of make-up.

Smiling at him, she said, "Colton, I want to show you the journal."

He heard her words and knew he needed to answer, but he was mesmerized with the vision she made.

"Colton?"

He gave her an awkward grin. He felt Frank staring at his back and knew that he had witnessed the whole thing. He felt like a teenager caught by his parents with his first crush. He was a grown man with a wall full of accommodations for bravery, yet this tiny female could turn him into a speechless bowl of mush!

She sat in the swing and patted the spot beside her. "Come sit with me."

He did as she asked; taking time to glare at Frank who left, grinning from ear to ear and saying he needed to make a phone call.

She opened the journal, and told him it had belonged to her ancestor Georgiana, who made the quilt. He watched her hands with the nails polished a pale pink, turn the pages slowly, until she came to the place she had written several paragraphs and signed her name.

"I need to write about what happened last night," she said as tears pooled in her blue eyes that had darkened with her grief.

Desperately wanting to spare her pain, Colton took her hands in his and closed the journal, laying it back in her lap.

"Not yet, Loren, I don't think it is time to write the final chapter."

His words made her pause. She was thrilled to hear him speak with such conviction. She wasn't sure Colton even realized it, but it was as if God had used his voice to convey a message to her. God was gently reminding her, through Colton, that it wasn't time to let go of her family legend. The face of the angel, surrounded with light that they had seen last night at the bayou, came to her mind.

She jumped up in excitement, and looked at Colton. Her eyes were rounded like the sea-blue pools of ocean. "Oh dear God, how could I forget! The angel! Maybe God sent us a sign of hope, to hold onto His Promise?"

She slipped into the shelter of Colton's embrace.

Thank You God, for renewed hope! And, thank You for using Colton to remind me that Your Promises are everlasting whether they are in heaven or here on earth!

Loren laid her head on his shoulder. Her heart was full of gratitude to God. He knew that she needed more than a physical and emotional attraction for the man who would capture her heart. She had to know, that he would trust her God and share the spiritual part of her life too. Colton had just proven that he knew that too.

Thirty-Eight

It was late afternoon, when the brightness of the sun had dimmed on the bayou, that Colton settled Loren, in the bow of the pirogue. He had said they would have a better chance of finding the quilt, without the glare of the sun on the water.

Standing in the center of the boat, he used the long pole in his broad hands, to push at the silt-covered bottom. Colton slowly moved the boat, along the shore in shallow water. He glanced at Loren. Her strained expression was mirrored on the dark water. She sat rigid, looking straight ahead. He knew she was trying not to look, at the spot where Jude had disappeared.

The slosh of the pole, entering the water, echoed across the surface. It was accompanied by the sound of bullfrogs, calling to each other as the sun slipped further out of sight. Colton maneuvered the pirogue close to the edge, moving in and out between the cypress knees jutting from the still water.

Loren leaned forward, desperately searching for sight of the quilt. "Do you see it," she asked hopefully.

He shook his head. He heard the silent cry in her voice, mingled with the mournful call of the night birds returning to their nesting places. Colton didn't remember ever feeling so helpless. He could put the nation's toughest thugs behind bars, but he was incapable of stopping the hurt he knew she was feeling.

The boat tilted as Loren stood. She excitedly pointed to a clump of trees, near the far edge of the bayou and cried out, "Stop! I see something!"

Colton looked in the direction she was pointing, and saw a light colored fragment of material snagged by the bark of the tree. The movement of the water rippled under the material, causing it to float away from its captor in an effort to break free.

He pushed the pole deeper into the soggy bottom of the bayou, inching the boat as close as he could without harming the boat. The trees formed a circle, with their roots spread out deep in the bayou, making them a dangerous risk to the bottom of the small boat they were in. Colton knew from experience, that sharp pieces of the tree could cut a gash in a boat large enough to sink it within seconds.

"I see it, Loren. I'll use the pole to drag it to us."

Holding her breath, Loren watched him tuck the long pole under the fabric, and slowly pull it away from the tree. He heart thumped in her chest as she watched him move it closer to the boat. When it was close enough to grab, Colton quickly reached for it, and put it in the boat at Loren's feet. She stared at the sodden fabric that was burned around the edges. She saw a line of buttons hanging at an angle. There was a large, gaping hole that was tinged an ugly black, close to where the buttons lay.

Colton knew what they had found before he saw Loren shrink back, cover her eyes and cry out in horror.

They had found a fragment of Jude's shirt, and it bore the evidence of the lightening strike that killed him.

He used his handkerchief to wrap the fabric, and then put it in his pocket. He pulled her trembling body close to him, and caressed her back slowly, giving here time to get past the ugliness she had seen.

"It's alright, Loren. I'm so sorry you had to see this. Let's go to the house, I need to call the sheriff. This is evidence they will need. I don't know how they missed this today. Maybe we'll have time to look for the quilt later."

She hid her face against his chest. The closeness helped to warm the chill that had settled over her. Seeing the tattered and burned scrap of material that she had seen Jude wearing last night shook her. It was proof that life is like a vapor, here one moment, and gone the next. If this was all that was left of him, chances were, there wouldn't be much left of the quilt either.

Thirty-Nine

Colton pushed the long pole against the bottom of the bayou, inching the pirogue closer to the Corbin's property. The tall trees with grey, Spanish moss hanging from their branches, cast weird shadows on the ripples the boat made in the water.

Just knowing that the scrap of Jude's shirt was in his pocket, made Colton feel like he was part of a funeral dirge that was carrying the last remains of someone. He looked at Loren, and stopped the motion of the boat for a minute. What he saw nearly broke his heart. Her head was bowed. Her shoulders were tensed. Colton thought she looked like she would break if anyone touched her.

"We're almost there, Loren."

She lifted her head to acknowledge that she'd heard him. Digging deep for her last vestige of strength, she laid her heart and her emotions bare, vulnerable and exposed before a man she'd known less than forty-eight hours.

"If someone had tried to show me a month ago the journey I was destined to take, I might have been tempted to refuse the offer. I've lost Gramma, who was my rock. I discovered a family legend; I met people who were connected through ancestors that were best friends, and I met you. God's destiny is an awesome way to live, Colton, but it can also be frightening when your faith is put to the

291

test. I am so humbled that each of you has chosen to walk this path with me."

The courage in her words found a spot in Colton's heart. As the boat glided to a stop on the marshy shore, he laid the pole in the boat and embraced her. He held her in his arms and let the rhythm of the water gently rock them. He caressed her hair, whispering soothing words, reminding her of what a brave women she was. How she had faced her demons without compromising her belief. And how she had stared down the barrel of a gun in the hand of a madman without flinching, and then had sacrificed a sacred legend, because of her desire to honor God and to protect her friends.

Somehow, he knew she needed to be reminded that Christians are not super humans. They are affected by all the things that life throws their way. They hearts can be disappointed, and broken. But, through it all, he had watched this amazing woman take on the challenges life had sent her way, without backing down. She could have turned her back, and walked away from her family legend. She didn't, and in his eyes, that showed tremendous bravery. He couldn't remember a time that he had been prouder of someone, than he was of Loren today.

Colton had never experienced such a flood of emotion towards another human being. He knew he was willing to do whatever it took, to secure her happiness. If this was true love, then he was in it for the countdown.

She raised her head from his chest. He caressed her arms and said, "Thank you, Loren for showing me there is more to life, than I'd ever imagined. I'll be here with you, as long as you want me to be."

Colton gently cupped Loren's elbow, and helped her from the boat. They stood on the shore a moment, then his fingers enclosed her small hand securely in his, and they walked slowly towards the house.

Loren marveled at the peace that came when Colton talked with her. Even at the spot where terror had pursued her just a few hours before, he was able to help her see beyond the awful horror that Jude had brought into her life.

Falling in love was such a wonderful experience. She didn't want them to rush past the enjoyment of this unfolding path that was leading into their future.

She smiled to herself as they walked, their clasped hands pulling them close to lean towards each other. She wondered why she had ever worried about meeting Mr. Right. It appeared that God had hand delivered him to her.

Forty

The crickets were singing their nighttime serenade, as Loren and Colton left the bayou. She looked at Colton's profile, tracing the strong lines of his features. She saw his mouth quirk at the corners. She realized he'd seen her stare, and blushed at having him catch her studying him so intently. He squeezed her hand. The sweet boyish gesture made her heart soar. Her pulse beat like war drums against the soft tissue of her wrists.

Contentment spread through her body. She felt a sense of intimacy with Colton that had nothing to do with physical contact. His nearness made her happy. She loved the kindness of his words - the way he looked at her - the gentleness of his voice. And, most of all she loved his growing faith in God.

Almost as if he could read her mind, Colton looked at Loren. He grinned, the smile devastatingly attractive. He came closer to her, the smile still in place; he stood toe to toe with her and studied her face before running his finger along her jaw. His touch was soft and intimate and words failed her. He bent closer as if he was going to kiss her. She waited for his mouth to descend, instinctively knowing it would be the best kiss of her life. A kiss that spoke of the way they had connected over the past two days. The way they could connect in the future.

They gazed into each other's eyes, oblivious to everything around them, until they heard a barking dog. They turned and saw Sam headed for the water with Frank right behind him in pursuit!

"Catch him! Don't let him get in the water," Frank yelled!

Loren and Colton ran after Sam, grabbing him just as his front paws touched the water. He yelped, wiggling his furry doggy body as he attempted to squirm out of their hands. He was determined to have an afternoon swim, but his captors held on firmly, just as determined to deny him the dip in the water.

Exhausted and out of breath from the headlong run down the sloping yard, Frank finally managed to say. "Thank you both. The way he's behaved after touching Loren's quilt, who knows, he might have tried to swim all the way across the bayou!"

The mention of Sam's earlier encounter with the quilt and its effect on him made Loren laugh. It bubbled up from inside her, replacing the disappointment and sadness she'd felt earlier when they'd found the burned piece of Jude's shirt. Her laughter was contagious, causing Frank and Colton to join her. They held onto Sam, who had given up trying to escape and was eyeing them with a suspicious glare. The sound of their laughter echoed on the still night air, until they were finally able to look at each other, without breaking out in laughter again.

Her eyes danced with humor. "Oh my goodness, God certainly knows his business when it comes to humans. Laughter is the best medicine! I believe he dumped the whole bottle in us!"

Frank nodded his head in agreement and snapped the dog leash onto Sam's collar. "No more races for you today, little man." Sam whimpered his disappointment, and then followed Frank without further comment.

When they stepped onto the porch, everyone was standing, grinning at the show the dog had put on. "Old Sam gave you all a run for the money," Emilie teased as Frank sat down in a rocker. He held on to Sam's leash, just in case he tried to make another escape to the water.

Colton came inside after he'd finished the call to the sheriff's office to let them know that they'd found a piece of Jude's shirt in the water.

"His shirt! Are you saying you found Jude's body," Frank asked.

"No, we just found part of his shirt. It was hung in the tree roots near the edge of the bayou."

Loren shivered at the memory of seeing the burned fabric. Colton saw her strained expression, and was attempting to get away from answering their questions, when the deputy arrived.

Frank and Colton saw his car pull to the back of the house and went out to meet him. Loren knew he was taking the burned piece of fabric to the deputy so that she wouldn't see it again. His kindness made her appreciate him even more.

When the deputy left, Emilie told Sailor to come inside with her to prepare a light supper. She teased Sailor.

"After the feast the girls made for us at lunchtime we'd best go with a snack so our stomachs can recover."

"Mama, that's not a nice thing to say."

"Aw, I'm just teasing, darling. The food was delicious," Emilie said as she hugged Sailor and walked behind her into the kitchen.

Loren offered to help, but Emilie told her to relax and enjoy her last night in Louisiana by listening to the music of the night sounds produced by the creatures of the bayou.

In the stillness, Loren laid her head on Colton's shoulder, who was sitting by her in the swing. Ms. Emilie was right, the night creatures played music. She felt the tenseness leave her body. Loren closed her eyes and allowed the high call of the marsh birds and the intermittent bass of the bullfrogs and gators to bring peace to her heart. Knowing that it was the right thing to do, she prayed that Jude had found forgiveness for his actions. Then she prayed that she could find the beauty in the bayou, without remembering the ugliness that Jude had brought there.

Her musing was interrupted by the slamming of the door, as Sailor closed it with her foot. She carried a tray laden with mile-high roast beef sandwiches, chips and dip. The delicious smell made everyone sit up straighter. They didn't hesitate to obey when Sailor told them Mama said for everyone to, 'dig in'.

As they enjoyed the food, Frank told them that Colton was going to drive him and Loren to Tallahassee tomorrow. "I'll leave the car here tonight and ride with Colt to his place."

Maurice told them he had talked with the director of the funeral home. "He said that Jude had made his own funeral arrangements several years ago. So if his body is found, he will be cremated and his ashes entombed in the family crypt in New Orleans."

The next half-hour was spent listening to Emilie talk about what it was like growing up in the backwater bayous. Her candor about how she should produce her life story of swamp-life, and make millions of dollars like some families were doing on television, had everyone agreeing with her ambition.

"You ought to do it, Mama. We'd call it *Em and Brim*. You could show folks how to fish and how to cook them after they caught them. You'd be a hit show in no time," Sailor encouraged her.

Maurice took Emilie's hand and said, "Well, before you turn into a big T.V. star, darling, us senior citizens need some sleep. You young folks can call it a night whenever you're ready."

"I'm in the senior division too," Frank laughed and stood.

"That's my clue that Frank is ready for bed," Colton said as he took Loren's hand.

Frank walked ahead of them to the truck. He and Sam crawled in the truck, and shut the door to give Loren and Colton privacy to say goodnight.

Lingering in the shadows at the side of the house, Colton turned to Loren and cupped her face in his hands. "I hope you sleep well tonight. I'll be here early tomorrow. We can go to the bayou to see if the quilt has drifted towards the shore. Is that okay with you?"

"Yes, that's what I need to do. Thank you for understanding."

"I'm pretty new at this believing stuff, but if God is as powerful as you said He is, then we need to give Him the time to work out His plan for the quilt by not losing hope."

"Oh, Colton, your heart is so open. You really do believe He can bring the quilt back to us, don't you."

"I figure that will be easy for Him. He brought you to me when I had just about given up on finding the woman of my dreams. Finding a quilt in the water, that'll be a piece of cake for Him."

Loren was so touched by the sincerity and tenderness in Colton that she just stood there, lost for words.

He grinned as if he understood what she was feeling. He hugged her a last moment, then stepped away. "Get some sleep. Goodnight, and don't let the bedbugs bite."

The familiar phrase warmed her heart as she watched him get in the truck, back down the driveway and pause to throw her a kiss before driving away.

She watched the taillights fade into the darkness before she returned to the porch where Sailor and Daughtry sat, quietly talking.

When Loren joined them, Daughtry said, "It seems impossible that less than a week ago we didn't know each other existed, or that you would bring a quilt to me that would forever change my life."

Tears pooled in her eyes at the mention of the quilt. "It has changed all of our lives. I am still amazed at how God led me to find you and Sailor. I am so thankful that God doesn't leave us alone down here on earth. He guides us with the inner voice of His Spirit. That doesn't mean that we get it right every time, but when we miss His voice, He will nudge us back towards the right decision if we allow Him too. I wish His plan hadn't included giving up the quilt that brought us all together."

"I know, Loren, but we still have our friendship and the wonder of knowing what we discovered about the seeds. We were all affected by its presence. In fact, everyone that touched it has been affected by it in some way. For right now, that is enough", Daughtry said.

"I suppose you're right. I just wish it could have been different."

"Loren, don't try to second-guess God. His plan will never fail, even when we cannot see how it will work out. That's what faith is."

"I always said you have great faith, Daughtry."

"And, I told you, we serve a great God. Let's get some sleep. Tomorrow is a new day. We need to be ready for what it brings."

Loren lay quietly in the dark room. She was amazed to find that the terror she had experienced at Jude's hands had lessened. She knew it was the peace of God. She was so grateful that Gramma had given her a Christian upbringing. But, most of all, she was thankful that she had made her own decision to follow Christ at an early age. All the right upbringing in the world doesn't mean anything, if you don't accept Him as your own Savior.

"Thank you, Jesus for the way you have guided me since Gramma died. Thank you for the people you have added to my life and for protecting them - they have become family. I had no idea that you would send me someone like Colton during one of my most trying times, but I want to especially thank you for him. Thank you for keeping Georgiana's quilt safe, wherever it is. Like Colton said, it is not lost to you. You know exactly where it is. Tomorrow is a new day; guide me I pray, in Your Name."

She drifted peacefully to sleep with hope in her heart that God would allow Georgiana's quilt to be part of her new day.

. . .

Loren shielded her eyes against the sunlight streaming through the curtains in the bedroom. She lay there, listening to the muted sound of voices carried from the kitchen to the bedroom where she was. The added smell of coffee gave her the momentum she needed, to shake off the covers, and get out of the comfortable bed. She'd slept well, and felt rested. Her thoughts were bittersweet, a part of her felt happy to be going to Tallahassee today with Colton. But, on the other hand, there was sadness at knowing she could be leaving the quilt in Louisiana.

She looked at her reflection in the dresser mirror, God, even if we don't find the quilt, You are still God, she thought, knowing that He heard her unspoken words. It's an awful position I find myself in, wanting to go, wanting to stay. The best I can do today is trust You, no matter what the outcome is.

Running a brush through her sleep-tousled hair, she heard Colton's deep voice say good morning. Her hand stopped the brush in mid-air. Suddenly, she had an overwhelming desire to look her best for the ride home. Rummaging through her meager assortment of clothing, she chose the only outfit she had not worn since she'd gotten here. It was a turquoise-blue sundress that she'd picked up on a whim when she and Sailor had shopped the discount store that Mr. Frank had stopped at in Alabama. Daughtry said he had left a couple pairs of jeans and shirts from his last visit, so he and Mr. Frank waited in the car while they shopped.

She slid the dress over her head and found that it fit to perfection. It was not what she'd call chic, but it made her sea-colored eyes sparkle and brought out the color in her porcelain skin. Taking just a little more time than usual, Loren applied a hint of makeup, and a spray of her favorite perfume that she kept in her purse. She straightened her reddish brown hair until it lay softly around her face. She closed her bag and placed it at the foot of the bed planning to take it to Colton's truck later.

Colton heard her footsteps and turned as she walked up behind him. "Wow! Look at you, all dressed up for me!" he teased.

Caught off guard by his teasing, Loren blushed at his comment, and went past him to take the cup of coffee Ms. Emilie offered her. The twinkle in Emilie's eyes brought a grin to Colton's face.

As they all sat at the patio table for their breakfast of toast and fruit that Emilie had served, Frank noticed that Loren glanced towards the bayou several times.

When they'd finished eating, he said, "If you bag is packed, Loren, I'll take it to the truck for you. Meanwhile, why don't you and Colton walk down to the bayou? Could be the quilt floated up to the edge during the night."

"Okay, thanks, Mr. Frank, I would like to take a final look . . . you know, just in case it's there."

Colton took her hand as they walked to the bayou. The grass was still damp and slippery from early morning dew, so they walked carefully down the sloping yard to the water's edge.

The memories of her experience at Jude's hands seemed at odds with the calm surface of the bayou today. She held her hand above her eyes, squinting against the early morning sun that danced across the water. She searched the bayou, willing the quilt to be there. It wasn't. The thought of never seeing or touching it brought sorrow that tore at her heart.

Colton stood close, his arm around her waist. He didn't speak as she searched every inch of the water.

Finally, she turned in his embrace. "It is so hard to believe it is really gone."

As soon as her words were spoken, the soft air around them sparkled with tiny pinpoints of light. They caught on the wind that carried the unmistakable smell of honeysuckle and rose in its currents. It lightly swirled around Loren and Colton.

All things are possible with God!

Colton leaned forward, a half-smile tugging at his mouth. Loren knew he had smelled the familiar fragrance and heard the reassuring words in his heart too. "Could be its not gone, just in a different place,"

"Could be, you are absolutely right," she said as she smiled back at him. She looked out across the bayou again. In the distance, the trees cast a reflection on the calm surface of the dark water. The breeze was warm against her skin, offering comfort in the very spot where they had experienced such horror, a short time ago. To Loren, it was a fitting place to take the next step on their journey, a spot that now spoke of hope. And tomorrow. And God.

Epilogue

"So much has happened since we traveled this road to Louisiana, it feels like it was weeks ago instead of three days," Loren said as she looked at Colton sitting beside her. He nodded his head, keeping his eyes on the road that was crowded with traffic.

Slivers of excitement ran up her body.

Oh, Lordy me, I'm falling in love with the man!

They were about a half-hour from Tallahassee, listening to the consistent snores that Frank and Sam had been making for the last hundred miles.

Colton grinned and took her hand in his. He squeezed it affectionately.

"Yeah, it feels like I've known you so long you should be an old lady by now," he teased.

She played along with his teasing. "Okay, mister, since I'm the old lady, listen to me. During the time you are in Tallahassee, I would like for us to visit Monroe. My best friend Carolyn and her husband, Zac live there and they want to meet you."

"We can do that. I would love to meet your friends, Loren."

"Well, you've got to remember, we're small town folk. Not big city folk like you."

Colton lifted her hand and brought it to his lips. He held it there, touching each of her fingers with deliberate slowness. Loren felt her heart tumble.

Lord this man has got me in a spin!

"I've been thinking, Loren. Maybe I would like to be a small town resident too. Do you think you'd be interested in helping me achieve that status?"

Before Loren could answer, Frank thumped on the back of the seat and said, "Pay attention, son, there's the Tallahassee exist. You were just about to miss it."

Colton's question hung between them as he turned off the Interstate. When they drove onto Thomasville Road towards Frank's neighborhood, he said, "Drop me and Sam at my house, and then take Loren to Leta's. It's just down the street."

Colton chuckled as he heard his former partner giving him instructions just like he did when they worked together at NYPD. He gave him a salute and said, "Yes, sir!"

Colton let Frank out at his house then drove slowly until Loren said, "There's Doug and Leta's house. The one with the big front porch."

He turned into the driveway and shut the motor off.

Colton looked at Loren and said, "I know you've got a lot on your mind. You can take all the time you need to answer but I want you to know one thing. I'm in love with you and if a small town is where you want to be, then that is where I want to be."

"I want to be where you are too."

He embraced her, holding her, needing to say more, but using the restraint that he knew she expected until they were ready to take their relationship further.

He wanted her, but he was wise enough to recognize that her emotions were bruised from the loss of the legend. She needed him emotionally as much as physically. It had to be right for both of them.

Moving away from her, he said, "One more thing is on my mind. I don't want to bring up painful memories, but I've been thinking about what happened when Jude went into the water. I've lived in Louisiana long enough to be familiar with thunderstorms. The storm was over. Then all of a sudden a cloud gathered as if a hand had put it there. The bolt of lightning that shot out of it was like a bullet from a gun. Then, just as quickly as it had come, it was gone and the angel was there."

Loren shuddered as the memory of Jude's death. "I know. I can still see what happened like it is burned into my memory. When he pointed the gun at me, I prayed that God would protect us, but I never dreamed he would die."

"Help me to understand. Do you think God killed him because he tried to take the quilt?"

"To be truthful, I wondered if God did it too. But, that doesn't line up with what Gramma taught me about God. He certainly has the power to destroy whatever or whomever he chooses to destroy, but we live in a time that God has given us free choice. I believe Jude's choice is what destroyed him. The lightning was just the weapon used."

"But, Loren, what about the angel, why was he there?"

Loren picked up the journal that was on the seat by her. She traced the pattern of embossed flowers on the cover and then hugged it to her heart.

"I believe he was there because of the choices my family has made. God knew our choice was to protect the quilt."

He saw the flicker of sadness in her eyes. "I know you wish that you still had the quilt."

"I do miss it, Colton. It is so sad that it's gone, and we may never know the ending of the story. I did all I could. It's in God's hands now."

Colton lifted her chin, caressing her cheek with his thumb. "Loren, you told me that God can do anything. If God still has a use for the quilt then I believe He will keep it safe."

She put her hand over his hand, touched by the tenderness in his voice and whispered, "Colton, you are right. We can't lose hope!"

He saw the excited sparkle in her eyes. He knew she was thinking the same thing he was thinking.

"I know what you're thinking, but it's impossible, Loren. We saw the quilt disappear in the bayou in Louisiana. We're in Tallahassee."

"You're absolutely right! But, that doesn't matter to God! He is everywhere!"

She opened the door of the truck and raced across the yard with Colton right behind her. At the porch she stopped, and Colton slammed into her, nearly knocking her to the ground.

She pointed toward the corner of the porch, "Colton, the angel! Do you see him?"

He looked in the direction that Loren was pointing. A brilliant light lit up the corner of the porch. The same angel they'd seen in Louisiana was standing where the roses and honeysuckle vines grew on the porch railing. They felt warmth cover their bodies like liquid gold as the angel looked into their eyes and smiled.

Unable to move, they held their breath and watched as the magnificent being from heaven slowly faded into the shadows of evening.

"He's gone, Colton," Loren whispered.

"Yeah, I wonder why . . ."

"Could it be? Oh, Lord, do you think . . . she muttered, dancing with excitement as Colton unlocked the door. She took his hand and pulled him towards the bedroom. She stopped and stared at the black leather chest on the table at the foot of the bed.

"Is that Georgiana's chest?"

"Yes," she whispered.

Colton said, "You taught me to have faith in God. Open it, Loren."

She faced him. He saw love shining in her eyes. "I want us to open it together, Colton."

Her words made him feel like he was finally home. He had dreamed, since he was a child, that one day he would have a family, but, he had just about given up on ever finding someone to share the dream with him. His heart pounded in his chest. Loren was offering him more than just a life with her. She was asking him to share the Promise that God had placed in her family nearly two centuries ago.

He caressed her arms gently and said, "I want to be a part of all your life, my darling Loren, including what God has entrusted your family with."

Loren laid her hand over his and they slowly eased the top of the chest up. The quilt lay there…as perfect as if it had been quilted that very day.

"It's there! The angel brought it to us!"

They lifted it out of the chest. Their clasped hands found the center of the quilt where Georgiana and Alice had placed the Promise. They felt the tingle run up their fingers, letting them know the seeds were still there.

The locked their arms around each other, holding the Promise between them. They stood quietly, content in the presence of God. The future lay before them, calling to them, assuring them that the God they served would guide them every step of the way. The rightness of the moment was blessed as the fragrance of rose and honeysuckle enveloped them. It foretold of a love that would last a lifetime and assure that a first-born daughter would once again inherit the Legend of Promise.

Acknowledgments

Writing is a solitary profession but it is not a lonely one, because I have so many people bouncing around in my head. They soon go from characters in my imagination to living, breathing people.

I live with them happily for months on end, creating their lives, and sharing in their problems and achievements.

By the time this book was finished they truly were real people to me; with lives that will live on in my memory and hopefully in the memories of those who read this story. Nothing would please me more than to know that I have done my job of creating these characters well enough that they become real people to you too.

I must mention all the people that have made the creation of this book so worthwhile. My husband Edward has listened to plot lines endlessly. My children, grandchildren and great-grandchildren have sacrificed two days of visits to our house each week so that I could write. All of them have watched this book consume me for the past year with only an occasional complaint.

My thanks go to Jason Taylor, a true computer whiz, who got everything onto the computer for publication.

I want to thank the girls, Jonnie Whittington, Sydney Clary, Toni Garland and Sheilah Broughton who make up Writer's INK, the greatest little writing club in the world. Their expertise to edit without judging has been invaluable. I am eternally grateful to each of you.

Last but certainly not least my thanks go to Jack Howdeshell, photographer extraordinaire, who managed to take the thoughts in my mind and create the perfect book cover.

It has been such an awesome journey; I do believe I'll do it again!

Coming in 2014

The enchantment continues with Book Two, *Gathering Promises*.

This spellbinding mystery wraps you more into the life that Loren and Colton choose as they continue their journey as husband and wife. They know that God has brought them together for this special time in history. They join forces a final time with Dr. Daughtry Corbin to learn the secret of the Promise that will reveal the power of God's provision for mankind.